Elfhame Academy Book 2

Tiffany Shand

Copyright © 2023 Tiffany Shand

All rights reserved. No part of this book may be reproduced in any form.

ACKNOWLEDGMENTS

Cover Design by Creative Cover Book Designs

CHAPTER 1

CASSIE

The first Drow lunged at me then a second one knocked me to the ground. The air left my lungs in a whoosh.

Murphy, my dragon, launched himself at the second Drow and clawed at him.

Fighting dark elves with no souls. Just an average day for the elf slayer. I leapt up and spun into a kick that knocked the first Drow away from me. Grabbing my sword, I sliced the head off the Drow and knocked the second one away.

"Are you gonna help?" I called out to Ash.

As my magus, it was his job to help me fight monsters that came out of the Nether Realm. Instead, my so-called helper lay back on a plastic chair with his hands behind his head. His short dark hair framed his handsome chiselled face and his blue eyes remained fixed on me.

How did he just sit there? Couldn't he see I needed help?

"Nope. I'm only here to observe. You're the one who's supposed to kill things." Ash flashed me a grin.

"You could fight them instead of just sitting there." I whacked the second Drow with my blade.

"That was a sloppy blow," Ash remarked. "You're supposed to kill them, not maim them."

"Yeah, yeah. You could get off your elven arse and help!"

The second Drow thrashed at me with his claws. They missed me by inches. I spun around and plunged the sword through his chest. Using a sword wasn't as easy as you'd think given the size of the blade.

Raising my hand, I threw a burst of purple light at it. The second Drow slumped to the ground and a third appeared and staggered after him when I hit him with another blast of magic. Damn, why couldn't my magic just blow him up? It would make things so much easier.

The third one regained his composure and lunged for me. I blocked his blow and sliced his head off. The head and the body fell to the ground with a thunk. Black blood covered me and the ground.

"Ugh, I'll need a good dry cleaner to get this stuff off me." I groaned. "Now almighty magus, can you help? Sending things back to the Nether is part of your job description."

Ash got up. "We can't afford to be sloppy." He wore his usual leather jacket, dark shirt and jeans.

"Hey, I'm better than I was a few months ago." My jeans and hoodie were covered in blood. No doubt blood would be congealed in my long, dark purple hair as well. "Told you I'd be damn good after some practice."

Ash frowned at me. "What is with your obsession with hunting every night? You're getting kinda bloodthirsty."

I laughed and leaned on my sword. "Ash, I've been out of the game for seven years. That's seven years without a slayer. Which means I have a lot of catching up to do."

"Cassie, you were twelve when your mum died. You wouldn't have become a slayer until you were at least fifteen."

"I'm not bloodthirsty. A few less Drow around keeps everyone safe." I bent and wiped my sword on the grass. That would probably need cleaning too.

"Sure you're not just angry about what

happened to your sister?"

I winced. Why did he have to bring that up? I didn't want to talk about my sister's death let alone think about it. Maybe slaying had been a good distraction, but nothing would bring Liv back. He knew I hated talking about what happened to my sister last term. Liv got herself mixed up with a necromancer and some pretty dark magic. That had cost Liv her life and affected a lot of other people, including me. Now everyone viewed her as a murderer. After everything I'd uncovered, I couldn't really deny the accusation anymore. That hurt almost as much as losing my sister.

"The Drow didn't kill my sister. Any luck tracking down information on the Queen of the Nether?"

I knew my sister had been searching for our birth mum's killer. That was why she got involved with a necromancer. She'd found the witch and learnt the Queen of the Nether had ordered our mum's death. Liv stopped the witch but had been killed herself trying to get into the Nether Realm.

"It's okay to talk about it." Ash put a hand out to touch my shoulder.

I brushed him off. "Don't. I'm covered in Drow blood. Besides, I'm fine." The last thing

I wanted to do was talk.

"Are you?" Ash arched an eyebrow. "I'm here if you need me. Bottling up your emotions isn't good for anyone."

"No, I'm covered in crap. Of course I'm not fine. Let's get out of here so I can get a damn good shower." I ran a hand through my long messy hair. "I'm not bottling anything up. Nor do I need to talk about it."

I had spent the last couple of months of the summer holidays working with Ash pretty much every day. We stayed in Colchester for a while, but I was needed more in Elfhame. It was closer to the Nether Realm than the human one. Ash rented a place for us to stay in so we got used to living together. That had taken some getting used to. Even though we were good friends he kept going on about Liv's death. That grew tiresome.

"Looking forward to going back to the academy?" Ash asked as we wandered away from the field.

My last term at the academy had been more about controlling my powers and learning what had happened to my sister. My powers were a lot more controllable and I'd found out the truth about Liv. I'd wondered if I should bother going back or not. But the place had more answers there about the

Nether and my mum's killer, so I couldn't afford not to go back.

"I guess. It will be good to see Lucy and Ivy again."

I'd missed my roommates. We had spoken and hung out a couple of times over the summer, but it wasn't the same as seeing each other every day and attending classes together.

Murphy flew alongside us, then plonked himself or my shoulder. His amber eyes shimmered like golden orbs and his silver scales shimmered like moonlight.

"Hey, you're getting too heavy for that." Murphy ignored me and wrapped himself around my shoulders. I shoved him off. "If you get covered in blood, I'll have to put you in the shower."

Murphy yelped and leapt into the air, then growled. He hated water and he took me threatening to bathe him as a punishment. It wasn't my fault he got covered in so much crap.

Tomorrow we headed back to the academy's island. The start of a new term and school year. I hoped it would be an improvement on the last one and with less training. Last term had been a blur of neverending classes, training with Ash and working on my sister's case.

Ash and I headed back to our flat. It wasn't much, but it gave us somewhere to sleep and chill when we weren't working. It had two small bedrooms, a lounge, kitchen area and a bathroom. The beige walls looked pretty bland, but we had managed to get some old furniture to make the place a bit more cosy. We mostly only slept here so we hadn't spent much time doing the place up. I'd taken a couple of classes over the summer. Just to get me more up to speed on elven magic. I'd be glad to move back into the North Tower and be with my friends again. Although I would miss being around Ash all the time. We had gotten used to living together pretty quickly and it would be strange not having him around.

After a shower, I changed clothes and found Ash in the living room feeding Murphy.

"Hey, fancy some dinner?" Ash asked.

I glanced at the clock on the wall. "Don't you mean breakfast? It's four in the morning."

"Okay, breakfast."

"I guess. Do you want me to order something or will you cook?" I gave him a hopeful look. He was the only one of us who could cook anything half decent. And I felt too exhausted to do anything.

"Order. I'm too tired to cook."

"Funny, given how you sat on your arse all night." I scoffed and slumped onto the sofa. "I'm the one that's knackered after doing all the fighting."

"Hey, I observed and got rid of them once you killed them. That's what a magus is supposed to do."

"Wow, my elf in shining armour." I rolled my eyes. "Pretty sure you are supposed to help with the fighting as well."

Ash headed over into the small kitchenette and took his phone off charge. "What do you fancy? Pancakes? Full English breakfast?"

"Pancakes sound good."

Ash called a local food delivery service then joined me on the sofa. It still surprised me the elves had agreed to such a thing like food deliveries. Usually they detested anything that humans did.

Before breakfast arrived, Ash and I fell asleep, my head resting on his shoulder.

The sound of the front door banging made me jolt awake again.

I jumped when I found a female elf glaring at me. "Who the fuck are you?" she demanded. She had long black hair, pointed ears and dark eyes.

"I'm Cassie. Who are you?" I reached for my sword that I had propped up against the sofa and grasped it tight. One thing I'd learnt since last term was to always have a weapon handy and to keep several weapons around the house. I never knew when I might be attacked by something. It was better to be prepared for anything.

The woman didn't look like a Drow or any other creatures I'd encountered so far but that didn't mean she wasn't an enemy.

"I'm Raisa. Why are you in Ash's flat?"

"Because I live here." I glanced over at Ash, who still lay slumped against the cushions with Murphy lying on top of the sofa.

Her eyes widened. "What? You live together? That son of a bitch!"

"Yeah. Why are you here?" I searched my mind for her name and thought back to if Ash had ever mentioned her. I thought Ash had mentioned her once as an old friend but couldn't be sure. "Do you break into people's flats all the time?" I kept a grip on my sword and braced myself for a possible attack.

She glanced down at my sword and her eyes widened further. "Unbelievable." Raisa stormed off and slammed the front door behind her.

Ash groaned. "What was that?"

"Your former friend with benefits was just

here. Didn't seem too happy." I'd almost forgotten about his former fling from last term. I'd never met her before so I didn't think she was someone that important to him.

"My what?" He rubbed the sleep from his eyes.

"Friend with benefits. Didn't look very happy to learn that I live with you."

Ash sighed. "We are not friends with benefits anymore. We just had fun."

"Your personal life isn't my business." I shook my head. "Bet you'll be glad to get rid of me, huh? Don't worry, I'll be out of here in the next few days."

He narrowed his eyes. "You're moving out? Why? You're welcome to stay here for as long as you need to. It's easier for us to live under one roof."

I shrugged. "Figured I'd move back in with my roommates. I thought you'd be glad to have the place to yourself again. It can't be easy for your dating life with me being around all the time."

He shrugged. "Guess I got used to you being here."

"There's not enough room for me and Murphy. I'll move my stuff out tomorrow. I better make sure I'm ready for the start of a new term. Let's just hope this one is a lot better than the last one."

CHAPTER 2

CASSIE

A knot of apprehension formed in my stomach as I waited outside Elfhame Academy for my friends to arrive. The giant grey stone castle loomed behind me like a foreboding sentinel. Its diamond pane windows stared out like eyes watching every movement I made. Its towers and turrets looked like they should have archers ready and waiting for an attack. Once the castle had been used as a fortress, back in the old days before the elves turned it into a place of learning.

Would my roommates be glad to see me? Or had last term been a fluke since we'd all been involved in Liv's case? I thought we formed a pretty close bond. Lucy and Ivy had been there for me in ways friends never had before. I found it hard to trust people. Yet going through complete hell had brought us all together. Neither of them cared about me being the slayer either.

"Cassie!" Lucy ran over to me and threw her arms around me. "OMG, I missed you." Her long dark auburn hair was pulled back in a high ponytail and her gossamer wings sparkled around her like glitter.

"I missed you too." I grinned and hugged her back. "Is Evie not here with you?" I had half expected Lucy's girlfriend to move in with us this term. Evie didn't attend the academy, but she could probably get a job here.

Lucy's smile faded. "No, she is spending the next few weeks in the Ever Realm working for Queen Silvy. I'm gonna be miserable without her." She pouted.

"Hey." My other roommate, Ivy Blue, waved as she ran over and hugged me. "Great to see you." Her long red hair fell over her face and her blue gossamer wings fell down her back like a cape.

Despite the academy originally only being open to elves, over recent years they welcomed other supernaturals. Including fae like Ivy and Lucy.

"You too." I returned her hug. "I missed you both. What have you been up to?"

"I've been travelling around the Ever Realm with Evie over the summer." Lucy grinned. "I'm gonna miss her while she's away."

Ivy shrugged. "I've been busy doing a science program and conducting new experiments. I'm hoping to get an apprenticeship with the Elhanan soon and become one of their research assistants."

"What have you been up to?" Lucy linked her arm through mine. "Still busy with slaying?"

I winced. "Keep your voice down. You know other people can't know what I am or what I do. And yeah, I have. I did some extra training over the summer as well. Come on, we should get moving. The assembly will be starting soon."

The academy always had an assembly to hail the start of a new university year and to welcome new students. We headed up the academy steps. Two massive gargoyles stood at the entrance and I half expected them to come to life and roar at me. Strange, I never thought the elves would be ones to go for gargoyles. But I knew gargoyles were meant to ward off evil so maybe that was why they had adopted them. Thankfully the statues remained silent.

"Are we getting a new dorm? Does anyone know?" Lucy asked as we headed down the corridor.

The oak floor gleamed and more statues lined the passageway along with portraits of different elves.

"I'd rather go back to the North Tower." Ivy pushed her long hair off her face. "It was perfect for us. At least no one bothered us there and we had much more space and privacy than we would have in a dorm room. I really don't want to go back to a normal dorm room."

I shook my head. "We still have the North Tower. I moved my stuff over there this morning. Guess the chancellor would prefer us to stay out of the way after what happened last term."

"You got here early?" Lucy furrowed her brow. "I thought they didn't let students on the island before noon?"

"I was already here. I've been living with Ash over the summer."

Lucy gaped at me. "Wait, what? You never said you and Ash lived together. When did this happen?"

I shrugged. "Not long after last term ended."

"So are you finally a couple?" She gave me

a hopeful look.

"No, of course not." I couldn't believe she jumped on that train of thought already. "We're not allowed to date. And even if we were, it would be weird given how closely we have to work together."

Last term, Lucy had been convinced Ash and I belonged together. The idea was stupid.

"You're allowed to live together." Lucy waggled her eyebrows. "Did you share the same room?"

"We had separate rooms." I scoffed. "Get your mind out of the gutter."

"Are you seeing someone else then?"

"No, I don't have time for romance." I rolled my eyes.

"You're not going to use your powers and the slayer excuse again, are you?" Lucy's frown deepened. "Come on, even you need to get some sometimes."

"Not everyone needs romance in their lives." Ivy scowled. "Some of us are happy being single. Besides, dating is a complete waste of time anyway."

"Right, says the girl who plays with primordial poo." Lucy laughed.

"Great, you two are bickering already." I groaned. "Luce, I don't want or need a boyfriend."

"Being in love is wonderful." She smiled. "I just want you to experience the same happiness. You deserve it after all the crap you went through."

"Right, your girlfriend is away for the next few months," Ivy pointed out. "You're overcompensating because you don't have your significant other in your life to keep you company. And you're projecting your insecurities onto us."

"Absence makes the heart grow fonder. So I'm gonna find both of you a boyfriend —" Lucy began.

Ivy glared at her. "No, you won't. I have explosives and I will use them. Even on you if you try to set me up with anyone, the last thing I want is a man in my life interfering with my work. Men are like utensils, you use them, wash them and then put them away until you need them again. Which in my case isn't very often."

"And I will slay you," I added. "Besides, why would I need a man when I have an adorable dragon?"

"But what about —" Lucy stopped when Ivy and I glowered at her. She raised her hands in surrender. "Okay, excuse me for trying to help."

"Neither of us needs romantic help," Ivy

insisted. "Why waste time on romantic nonsense? It would only get in the way of my work and Cassie's work."

"Really? Because you sure as hell need to —" Lucy said.

"Guys," I hissed, as we headed into the great hall and they finally both shut up.

The great hall spread out with its high vaulted ceiling, gleaming oak floor and whitewashed stone walls. Flags hung overhead depicting the different elven houses and swayed gently back and forth. Large rows of wooden benches encircled the room and seemed to reach to the ceiling. A row of chairs stood on a dais at the front of the room along with a podium where the teachers usually sat along with the chancellor.

We took our seats on one of the upper rows. This time last term I'd been a newbie as had my roommates. It felt strange to see a bunch of new people in the first years' section. But it would be good to not feel like a newbie anymore. I just hoped the elves wouldn't torment any of us the way they had last term.

One woman with purple and turquoise hair stared up at me from where she sat in one of the lower rows of benches.

Holy crap. Avery Devlin. I couldn't believe

she'd come here.

I waved and she grinned. One by one more students lined the rows of benches. The fair haired or dark-haired elves seem to congregate in the centre of the room whilst the rest of the hall filled up with a mixture of shifters, witches and fae. Different races tended to stick with their own kind.

The chancellor stepped up onto the dais. Her long blonde hair was pulled back in a plait and her ivory skin glistened like moonlight. She wore a stylish designer grey trouser suit and heels. "Welcome to a new term at the academy, students. I'm sure we're all eager for the new year and a new start."

"Is there gonna be more monsters like last term?" someone called out.

I couldn't make out who it was in the crowd of heads. Wait, why did someone have to bring that up? I'd make sure no monsters bothered anyone this term. That was my job as a slayer.

The chancellor's smile almost faltered and her gaze shot towards me. She was one of the few people on the island who knew about me being the slayer.

"Monsters come out of the Nether Realm on occasion. It's nothing to worry about," the chancellor insisted. "The island is well protected by the enforcers."

I snorted. Right, the enforcers who monitored things. Most of them didn't fight monsters, though. That was my job.

Plus, the enforcers refused to let me work with them, officially at least. The elven council hadn't been happy to find out about my true heritage. None of them wanted me here, but they didn't have much choice in the matter. My biological father pulled some strings to get me a place at the academy — on the condition I learnt to control my powers. And keep monsters in check. I'd done that. Hopefully they'd leave me alone. The chancellor only let me stay because of who Cal was. Like it or not, they needed me.

"We've heard there's a slayer here too. Is that true?" someone else demanded.

Great. Just bloody great! Well, I knew it couldn't stay a secret forever. Sooner or later someone would notice things and put two and two together. I just hoped it wouldn't interfere with my actual slaying. I had enough crap to deal with last year because of Liv's case and I didn't have time for it to interfere this term. I just wanted a normal year without all the drama of last term. Was that really too much to ask for?

The chancellor pursed her lips and her gaze

went to Cal, who glared at her. "Those are just rumours. Everyone on this island is safe."

"What about the other students?" Elora Elmese, an elven princess, spoke up. "Some of them are murderers and they blew up their housing block." She shot a pointed look towards me and my roommates.

"It was one room," Ivy muttered under her breath. "Why can't they just get over that already? Plus, it was a life-or-death situation."

I cringed, remembering how she'd blown up our dorm when a Drow attacked us. That nearly got us all expelled.

The chancellor moved on and the sorting began where first years got tested to find out what classes suited them. My sorting had been pretty dramatic last term. I was glad I didn't have to go through that again.

Once the sorting was over my friends headed out to go to the North Tower to start unpacking all of their stuff and get the place ready for our new term at the academy.

I lingered and looked around for Avery. It would be good to catch up with her again. I hadn't spoken to her in almost a year. We had fallen out of touch since I left Colchester to come to the academy. I had no idea she would be here. The last time I saw her she insisted she wanted nothing to do with magic anymore and wanted to live a normal life by keeping a low profile away from other supernaturals.

Odd. Where had she disappeared to? I half expected her to wait around for me so we'd have a chance to talk before she went off to her housing block. At least I assumed she'd be a student. Or maybe she'd got a job here. People weren't allowed on the island unless they worked or studied here. The elves were pretty strict with their rules.

I took out my phone and sent her a quick text message asking her where she was. I presumed her number was still the same. To my disappointment, no sign came through that she had read the message.

"Hey, I can't believe they let the murderer's sister come back," someone called out.

Oh, wonderful. So much for not being harassed this term.

I turned around and spotted a group of male elves. The same bunch who had harassed me last term. To my surprise, there was a girl among them this time. Poor cow. How stupid did you have to be to hang out with the likes of these guys?

Smiley and his cronies, who picked on Lucy a lot last term, sauntered my way.

Great. Just great. I so didn't have time for this.

Murphy had flown off and followed the others too. So he wouldn't be much help.

"Guess I didn't hit you hard enough last term." I blew out a breath. They attacked me on my first day last year. Some quick thinking had soon convinced them to back off. I wasn't about to let anyone push me around nor was I in the mood for their crap.

"We don't want killers on our island," Smiley — I had never bothered to learn his real name — growled at me and grabbed my arm. He had tanned skin, short black cropped hair and pierced pointed ears.

I shoved him backward and threw a burst of light at his head. It missed him on purpose and he yelped. "Leave. Me. Alone," I snapped. "Next time I won't miss."

"Get her!" Smiley yelled. He and his cronies advanced towards me.

I raised my hand, power pulsed through the air. All of them froze in place. "You're lucky I'm in a good mood. Or I would so have fun kicking your sorry arses."

Too bad me scaring them wouldn't get them to stop and finally leave me alone once and for all. No doubt they would come after me again, but they were more of a nuisance than a real threat.

I ran off and ducked down an alleyway

between some buildings. I headed to the main office to make sure I had an updated copy of my schedule for this term. Luckily my schedule was flexible in between classes due to the need for slaying and extra work. I picked up Lucy and Ivy's schedules as well before heading back out. I just hoped Smiley and his cronies wouldn't be lying in wait for me again. Hopefully I spent enough time in the main office not to run into them again for a while. I could report the harassment, but I knew it wouldn't do any good.

Ducking into a nearby alley, I spotted Avery up ahead. Finally, I'd half expected her to see her in the main office.

"Hey, wait!" I called out.

She glanced back at me then carried on walking. "Come on, Cassie." She motioned for me to follow her.

"What are you doing?" I ran to catch up with her. "Avery, where are you?" I rounded the corner which stopped in a dead end. A brick wall stood between the buildings. "Avery? Where did you go?"

She couldn't have just disappeared or maybe she could. I didn't think she used magic anymore. I met her when she had been involved in one of my mum's cases. She had vowed to stop using magic. Maybe that had changed since she'd come to the academy.

"Avery?" My senses went on alert. She'd wanted to talk to me. Or at least I thought she had. Why else motion for me to follow her? Why would she vanish on me? I thought she wanted to talk.

Then I spotted the body of Smiley lying face down on the ground.

What the hell? How the heck had he wound up here?

I knew I'd be in deep shit for this

CHAPTER 3

ASH

The last thing I expected was for Cassie to call and tell me she found a body.

I hurried out to meet her in an alley close to the castle on the main campus. The smell of dampness and rubbish hit my nostrils as I headed further down the path.

"What happened?" I asked when I found Cassie standing at the end of the alleyway near a brick wall.

"I don't know. One minute I was following my friend, the next he wound up dead." She shrugged. "I don't understand — he was frozen earlier."

"Wait, you used to your magic on him?" I furrowed my brow at her. I hadn't expected her to get into trouble before the new term even started.

"Yeah, him and his cronies attacked me. So I froze them and scarpered. But my magic probably wore off whilst I was in the main office getting class schedules. I thought he would be long gone by the time I came out of the office."

"Are you sure he didn't follow you?" I knelt beside the body and gave it a quick once over.

She crossed her arms. "Yeah, I think I'd remember that. I didn't sense anyone following me."

"Okay, who were you following?"

"My friend, Avery, but she disappeared."

The name didn't ring any bells. "Who?"

"Avery Devlin — I think she's a new student here. I followed her into the alley and found him." She motioned to the body.

"And where did she go?"

"I have no idea. She just vanished. And before you say anything, no. She can't be the killer. Heck, I didn't even expect to see her on the island. The last I heard she'd given up practising any kind of magic."

"I thought you were gonna work on not judging things before you had the facts this term?" I examined the body but didn't find any signs of injuries. "I wish you weren't the one who had found him. I need to find your friend and talk to her after I report this."

"I'm not —" She gritted her teeth. "I don't see how she had time to kill him. She was here and gone pretty damn quick. Besides, I know her. I don't see why she would need to kill anyone. Even him." Cassie motioned to the body again.

"You thought that about your sister," I wanted to say but didn't as I knew it would upset her. Everyone was capable of killing given the right circumstances. That much I knew. "You didn't touch the body, did you?" I said instead.

"No, of course not. My mum was an enforcer. I know not to touch anything at a crime scene." She pulled out her phone to check it. "I tried calling Avery, but I wouldn't be surprised if she's got a different number."

I pulled out my phone. "I'll have to call this in. The chancellor's gonna flip out when she hears this. Especially with your involvement. Why can't you stay out of trouble for five minutes?"

Cassie snorted. "It's not like I asked to find a dead body, Ash. He may have been a pain in the arse, but I didn't want him dead."

The chancellor hadn't been happy to find out Cassie was a slayer. But I knew I couldn't keep her name out of this case. Not for long at least "Have you called anyone else and told them about this?"

Cassie shook her head. "Just you."

"Okay." I called Cal and waited.

Cal Thornton, my boss and chief of the enforcers, appeared a couple of minutes later. To my surprise, he didn't bring anyone with him. Odd, I expected him to arrive with a full team to start assessing the scene. "What happened?" He was a tanned skinned elf with short dark hair, piercing blue eyes and he always wore sharp, designer suits.

Cassie gave him a rundown of what she had told me. I knew she wouldn't be happy to see him. She and her biological father had a complicated relationship and had never really gotten along.

"Looks like he died around the time Cassie last saw him," I remarked. My senses told me he hadn't been dead long. "Can't see any visible signs of injuries, though."

"You need to leave. Now," Cal told Cassie. "I'll keep your name out of this for as long as I can."

Cassie's blue eyes widened. "Wait, what? Why?"

"Because your involvement will cause more issues. I have been fighting to get you added to the Elhanan as a consultant. That won't happen if you're a murder suspect. Especially not after everything that happened with your sister. It's been hard enough convincing the other elves to let you anywhere near the Elhanan."

"My sister —" Cassie gritted her teeth. "Fine, I'll go. But keep me updated on this." She gave me a pointed look then stalked off.

"Not sure if you can keep her name out of this," I remarked. "Are you sure that's wise? She's a witness."

"She's still my daughter. I'll keep her safe whether she likes it or not."

Cal kept his distance from Cassie. She thought he didn't care about her but I knew that wasn't true.

"Other witnesses might have seen her. Cassie and I checked around and didn't see anyone."

"Witnesses see a lot of things. Besides, I know this elf and I know he and his friends were tormenting her. I won't have her true identity revealed."

"I can't see any visible injuries." I motioned to the body. "He must have been killed by some kind of magic."

"What do you sense?"

"Dark magic. My demon side senses it." Cal and Cassie were two of the only people who knew I was part demon. Something I never wanted other people to know.

"Yes, I sense it too. We'll need to run some tests to find out what killed him. I'll keep this quiet for now. People are already uneasy after everything that happened last term."

"You can't keep this a secret for long, boss. Something bad's gonna happen this term. I can feel it."

A team soon arrived and swept over the scene. Cal and I watched them as they got to work.

"Cal, did you mean what you said about Cassie working with us as a consultant?"

He nodded. "Of course. The slayer is a valuable asset. And she's your partner. I just hope she's ready. Emotionally, I mean. How's she doing?"

I shrugged. "She says she's fine after…everything that happened with her sister."

"Is she?"

"Somehow, I doubt it. I don't think you should bring her in. Not yet at least." As much as I would enjoy having Cassie working with me, I couldn't be sure of her emotional state. She was good at hiding her true emotions.

"You don't think she's ready. Your

accounts of her slayings have been interesting."

"Right, she's lost a lot, Cal. I'm not sure she can handle this. Working on a murder investigation might bring bad memories for her. I'm not saying she's not a good investigator because she is, but I don't want to push her too far."

"Are you ready to work your first case then?"

I gaped at him. "Are you serious?"

"You passed your training and even became a certified magus over the summer. I think you're ready."

I nodded. "I am. But with Cassie's involvement —"

"I know you, Ash. You don't let your emotions get in the way. Plus, this is what I've wanted all along, you and Cassie working together. Just like Estelle and I did." Cal looked away at the mention of Estelle's name. He'd loved Cassie's birth mum and never got over her death.

I headed off once I'd done a sweep of the scene and a team finally showed up to examine everything and take the body away. Then went back to the enforcers tower. I found my friend and fellow enforcer, Tye, in his lab. I'd seen him briefly at the scene before he disappeared again.

"I got my first case. Did you take samples?" I asked him as I headed inside the lab. Everything was sterile, white and chrome from the floor and ceiling to the equipment.

"Congrats, mate. Yeah, of course I took samples." Tye's blue-black hair was tied back in a long ponytail behind his prominent pointed ears. He wore his usual scuffed jeans, Metallica T-shirt and a white lab coat.

"Have you found anything?"

He laughed. "I'm not a miracle worker, Ash." Tye shook his head. "It's gonna take some time."

"Cal wants this case wrapped up and fast."

"Nothing unusual there then. I'll run the tests but the body looked weird. I'll have to do a post-mortem to see what I can find. The body should be on its way over soon." As he spoke, the double doors open and a couple of elves brought a trolley with a body bag in. "Here's the body of Vikram Tomar. This should be interesting. We haven't had any murders on the island for a few years."

Only he could be excited about this case. For me, I knew it would be a complete nightmare. Especially when the other elves heard about the news of Tomar's death.

"Right, call me when you have anything."

I knew where Vikram Tomar's friends liked to hang out in the food court so I headed there after leaving the tower. They all spent more time at the food court than they did at their classes or in their dorm rooms. All five of his cronies tensed as I headed over. I flashed my enforcer badge and clipped it onto my jeans. "Hey, I heard you lot got into trouble earlier."

"Hey, if the purple haired freak or that girl reported us —" the first one said.

"No, if you mean Cassie, she didn't report you. And what girl? Did you see someone else?" I feigned ignorance. All of them fell silent. "Listen, I'm not here because you tried picking a fight with Cassie. I'm here because your mate Vikram is dead." All of them gaped at me.

"How?" the second one asked. "We just saw him earlier."

"But that purple —" the third guy said.

"She's been questioned already. And we're still determining cause of death," I told them. "Did you try and jump her?"

"No, she did something to us," the first one said. He was a dark blonde-haired elf with a mousy face and goatee.

"Like what? Did she hurt you?" Cassie had

mentioned getting into a fight with them. But it wouldn't be the first time she'd faced off against Vikram's gang.

"She threw light at Vik."

"Did she hurt him?" My heart pounded in my ears. If Cassie had got into a fight, that would make things much more complicated than just her finding the body.

"No, just gave Vik a warning after he grabbed her. Then she did something else and disappeared. That freak has some weird magic. It's like she can stop time and disappear."

"Did you try and chase her?"

"No, Vik told us we'd get her later and left," the second one, another dark-haired elf with pale skin, spoke up.

"Did you see him harm her, then?" It would be different if she attacked Vikram in self-defence. She had thrown magic at him before, but I didn't think she would have outright hurt him in any way. Not unless she had to.

"No, man, we —"

"All of you will need to come and make statements at the tower."

"What, now?" the first one whined.

"Yeah, or you can do it here."

They opted for the second option and all

gave statements. I headed off to speak to more people who might have been potential witnesses. No one else seemed to have seen anything.

Then I did a search for Avery Devlin. She was the next person to question. I looked up which housing block she had been assigned to and drew a blank. Odd. Did she have housing somewhere else? Everyone who went to or worked at the academy lived on the island. There was too much security around for people to come on and off the island every day. I did another few searches and Avery's name didn't show up on any student, staff, or enforcer lists.

That didn't make sense.

After leaving the academy's main campus, I used a transportation stone to teleport over to the other side of the island to the North Tower. The large grey stone tower loomed like a silent sentinel.

I knocked on the heavy wooden front door and headed in, not bothering to wait for a reply. They usually told me to come in anyway. I knocked out of courtesy. Boxes were piled up all over the place and stuff was discarded everywhere.

"Ivy, come clean up your mess," Lucy yelled as she came through into the kitchen with her arms full of fabric.

The kitchen had whitewashed walls and a couple of scuffed marble countertops and old wooden cabinets. More boxes were piled everywhere full of kitchenware and bags of groceries.

"Need a hand?"

"Oh. Hey, Ash. Good to see you. No, not unless you know how to hang curtains." Lucy stumbled under the weight of the heavy fabric.

"Not exactly. Plus, I'm here to see Cassie." I needed to talk to her about Avery. Not waste time helping out with DIY jobs.

"Ah, that's so sweet. You miss her already?" Lucy smiled.

"Yeah. I mean, no." I shook my head. "I need to talk to her about the case."

"What case?" Lucy dropped the curtains. "Tell me."

"Er... No case." I didn't know whether to be relieved Cassie hadn't told her anything about Vikram's death or not. Damn, I should have been more careful. Now it would only lead to unwanted questions.

Lucy shook her head. "You're not a good liar, Agent Rhys."

"How do you know that?" I crossed my arms and frowned at her.

"Cassie told me how to tell if you're lying. So what's the case?"

"I can't tell you. You're not working with the enforcers. And you're not a trained informant either."

"No, but I'm top of my classes. Well, most of them. Come on, I'm good with research and I already know Cassie's big secret. So let me help." Lucy gave me a hopeful look. "A good enforcer should use all the resources at their disposal, right?"

"No, Cal would never agree to that."

"Cal doesn't need to know."

"I'm not gonna lie to him."

Lucy rolled her eyes. "Cassie's right, you are a stickler for the rules. I'll probably just get details from her anyway so you might as well tell me."

I shook my head. "Not gonna happen. Cassie shouldn't be talking to you about enforcer stuff."

Lucy rolled her eyes again. "It's not like I'm going to talk about the case to anyone else, Ash. I'm not that stupid."

Cassie finally came in. "Hey, have you found anything?" she asked me.

"No. Can we talk somewhere more private?" I rubbed the back of my neck.

"You can talk with me around," Lucy

remarked. "Heck, maybe I could help out on the case. Does it involve dark elves? Or has something been stolen? What is it?"

Cassie waved a hand in dismissal. "Go and hang the curtains up. I will go around and set some more wards later. We need to make sure we have plenty of protection in place in case Ivy blows up anything again."

Lucy scowled. "We need some more house rules. Why does she need to conduct experiments here in the tower? She should keep her work limited to a lab. We'll get expelled if she blows up another building."

"Hopefully, no one'll expel me since I'm the slayer and all. Now go and put up the curtains."

"That will only happen if one of us figures out how to use power tools." Lucy snorted then sauntered off.

"Are you sure you don't want to move back in with me?" I asked, half joking.

She shrugged. "I'll be okay here. Besides, this place is much bigger than your flat. What did you wanna talk about?"

"Are you sure you saw Avery?" I asked. "Because I can't find any record of her on this island."

"Yeah, I'm sure. She was at the assembly and outside in the alley. She waved at me when we were in the great hall. Why else would she be here if she wasn't attending the academy?"

"Who's Avery?" Lucy stuck her head around the kitchen door again.

Damn it, I should have known she'd be listening. So much for keeping this case under wraps. But then again, I trusted Lucy and I didn't think she would go blabbing to other people about the case. I just didn't want this case taken away from me. Cal liked enforcers to stick to the rules no matter what.

Cassie turned back to her. "Do you remember seeing someone me wave at someone in the assembly?"

"No, why?" Lucy remarked. "What does this girl look like?"

"Goth girl, with short pink and turquoise hair. She has a long arm sleeve tattoo of dark ink and a skull on her vest," Cassie explained. "You must've seen her. She's pretty hard to miss. She's a witch, not an elf."

Lucy shook her head. "I don't remember seeing someone like that. I think you waved at someone, but I didn't see anyone wave back. I was too busy watching the new students."

"But I saw her and spoke to her outside the castle. Why's there no record of her?" Cassie pulled out her phone and tapped away on it then scowled. "Maybe you missed something. Damn, you're right. But that doesn't make sense. Why else would she be here?"

"Maybe it wasn't her you saw," I suggested.

"Ash, I know what Avery looks like." Cassie tapped her phone again. "Wait while I call her…" We all waited for a few seconds in silence. "Damn, she's still not answering."

"Maybe you saw someone else or —"

"I can't believe you don't believe me." Cassie shoved her phone in her pocket and crossed her arms.

"I said it's weird we can't find any trace of Avery. Not that I don't believe you. But we better find out who killed Vikram before anyone else gets hurt."

CHAPTER 4

CASSIE

I had no idea why Avery hadn't shown up on any records. It made no sense as I knew I'd seen her. Had Avery disappeared? And why wouldn't she answer my calls? Or messages?

I wanted to focus on the case, but classes started in the morning. So the case would have to wait until later. Besides, it didn't seem like Ash wanted my help that much.

First up was history class. Lucy and Ivy had it with me.

"Since when do you study history?" I asked Ivy as we headed to the main campus.

The grey stone castle loomed over us like a silent sentinel. Most classes were held in the castle but more advanced larger classes were held in different places around the island.

"History's a good thing to learn," Ivy

replied as she swung her backpack over her shoulder. "Plus, it's one of my required classes so I've got to take it whether I want to or not."

"Yeah, especially given the stuff you play with," Lucy remarked. "With it being primordial poo and all." She snickered under her breath.

Ivy scowled at her. "That was one time! I experiment with a lot of different stuff. I don't play with anything."

The sound of their usual bickering didn't bother me. Small groups of students stood in the hallway all staring at their phones and whispering to each other. I wondered if news of Vikram's death had already spread across the academy.

I sat down at the table with them. The castle's familiar grey stone walls felt like coming home. I pulled out my phone and scrolled through it.

"Put that thing away," Lucy hissed. "You've been checking it all morning. Besides, you know you're not allowed to use that in class."

"I'm waiting for Avery to contact me." Since we had a few minutes before class began, I brought up Avery's social media accounts. Weird. She hadn't posted anything in months.

She'd been living under the radar for the last few years after she lost her family to creatures from the Nether Realm. Avery had asked my mum/aunt for help and Mum had helped her start over. I felt guilty over what happened to her. Even though I couldn't do much at the time.

Things were different now I was the slayer.

I toyed with the idea of texting my mum and asking her if she'd had any updates on Avery recently. But Mum wasn't stupid. She'd ask questions if I started asking around about Avery. Then she'd find out about the case. I didn't want her to know someone had been murdered or she'd only worry. Or worse she might come to the island herself and try to get involved. Although Mum wasn't a huge fan of the elves, she had worked as an enforcer alongside them in the past.

"Cassie, put the phone down." Ivy glowered at me. "We're on thin ice with the chancellor already. You need to at least look like you're participating in class."

"Ash is working the case, remember?" Lucy asked. "You're not supposed to be involved."

Blowing out a breath, I shoved my phone into my pocket. Searching for Avery would have to wait until after class.

Our history teacher, Francesca Aveline, came in. She was a tall, willowy blonde elf who always wore floral dresses. "Good morning, class. I'm sure you're all excited for the new term."

Groans rang out through the room. Lucy clapped, grinning.

I rolled my eyes. Only she would be excited about classes. Ivy would be excited about getting back into the lab. All I could think about was finding Avery and talking to Ash again. I hated not living with him now. Even though I knew time apart would do us both good.

My phone vibrated, I pulled it out and found a message from Ash.

It read: *No news yet. Cause of death is undetermined.*

Gritting my teeth, I shoved my phone back into my pocket.

Want to run some tests together? I asked Ivy in thought.

Me? Do tests on a dead body? Ivy cringed. *Gross. I don't touch dead bodies.*

It's to find out what kind of magic killed Smiley. Besides, you experiment with explosives. A dead body isn't that big of a deal. It's not like it can wake up and attack you. Don't you touch dead things in the lab?

Not dead elves. Smiley? Ivy furrowed her brow. *Who the hell is Smiley?*

The dead bloke.

I guess I could take a look. As long as he doesn't wake up and attack us. You're a slayer. Anything can happen around you.

"Do you girls actually want to be in this class?" Professor Aveline came over and demanded.

I jumped. "Yeah, sorry." Jeez, did she have to scare us like that? How did she even know we were talking to each other in thought?

Ivy blanched. "Of course we do."

"Good, then save the gossip for the food court." The professor approached the whiteboard and scribbled something onto it. "In today's class we're going to be talking about the history of elven warriors. Starting with the history of the most powerful warriors: slayers."

My mouth fell open. What the hell? Why did she choose to talk about that for the first class of term?

I couldn't fathom why. Did she suspect something? Did she know my true identity?

Maybe I should make a run for it. If I skipped class, I could help Ash with the case.

Lucy kicked me under the table when she

saw me glance towards the door.

Don't go anywhere. Slayers are part of elven history.

But —

Chill out. You can't start skipping classes or you'll flunk out of college. Besides, this should be easy for you. Don't you already know all this stuff?

"Elven slayers are one of the oldest warrior clans. Some say even before the elves became divided by a dark and light. Slayers fought things that came out of the Nether Realm," Professor Aveline said. "Does anyone know who the first slayer was?"

"Slayers are a myth," Elora scoffed. "What's the point in learning about them? They're just an old elf tale made to scare children into not misbehaving."

"No, they're not. Slayers have been around for millennia," Professor Aveline said. "They are considered the most powerful of all elven warriors. Once, there were many of them. It's unfortunate a lot of them were killed over the past few centuries. The goddess knows we were all much safer when there were more slayers around. Now, who can tell me who the first slayer was?"

"The first slayer was Cassandra of Misthaven," I spoke up. At least knowing some of the answers about slayers would help me get over my embarrassment from earlier. I'd been named after the first slayer.

"Very good. Cassandra was the first slayer. Everyone from her clan viewed her as a powerful and fierce warrior," Professor Aveline went on. "What's the slayers' creed?"

"We are the light in the shadows," I said without thinking. "I mean, slayers are." Jeez, I needed to be more careful.

"You seem to know a lot about slayers." The professor arched an eyebrow at me. "Are you any relation to the McGregor family? Are any of them still slayers?"

Holy crap, why was she asking so many questions? Did she know what I was? I bit my lip. "I'm a Morgan, not a McGregor." That was true enough. Mum changed my last name when she officially adopted me after my birth mother's murder. Mum had also changed her own name from McGregor to Morgan as she wanted to separate herself from the McGregor family name.

If she only knew, Lucy remarked.

I kicked her under the table.

Don't make her any more suspicious of me. The less people that know about me the better.

I breathed a sigh of relief when class was finally over. "Do you think she suspects I'm a slayer?" I asked as we headed out.

"She will if you keep answering all those questions," Ivy remarked. "You didn't even give anyone else a chance to answer."

Lucy waved a hand in dismissal. "I know some of the answers too. The information is all available if you want to find it. Plus, I doubt most of the people in class would even pay attention to slayers. Some of the elves think you're just a myth."

"I have to get samples from the enforcers tower. I'll meet you both at the magical arts tower," I told them and headed off.

I knew getting samples from the tower would be risky. Ash would never agree to give them to me willingly. The enforcers tower loomed like a dark shadow. All dark stone and tall windows that stared down like empty eyes. At least the castle didn't have a foreboding feel about it. But this place had never been designed to be welcoming. It was a place of justice, law and order.

"Hey, any news?" I found Ash at his desk.

I still snickered at the idea of him having a desk, but all enforcers had to fill out paperwork. At least I didn't have to put up with that with being a slayer. Any paperwork we had was usually handled by my magus.

"Nothing." Ash sighed. "I can't find any

CCTV footage of where Vikram was killed. So no sign of him or his killer going into that area."

"I haven't been able to get hold of Avery either."

"We do have you and Vikram's gang on CCTV earlier," Ash said. "No sign of anyone else. Are you sure you saw Avery? Maybe it was someone who looked like her."

"Of course I'm sure. She spoke to me."

"Cass, there's no evidence to show her coming onto the island," Ash said. "People can't just teleport here. They have to have approval or the island's magic would prevent them from setting foot here."

"I know what I saw, Ash. I couldn't have imagined it."

"Was Murphy with you?"

"Only in the great hall. He flew off after that." Murphy perched on my shoulders, half asleep. "Have you got a cause of death yet?" I glanced over at Tye.

Tye stood at his desk tapping away on his keyboard. "I've got nothing. I've been running dozens of tests."

"My friend Ivy could help you out. She's really good with testing different magics."

Tye shook his head. "No can do, slayer. Your friend has a record. She can't be associated with us. We can't take the risk or the case could be thrown out if we catch a possible suspect."

"But she could help," I insisted. "Don't you want to find the killer before someone else gets hurt?" I'd never understand the enforcers and all of their ridiculous rules. Sure, there needed to be rules and laws in place, but the elves had so many edicts it was a wonder they ever got anything done.

"It was probably a hate crime given what an arsehole he was," Tye remarked. "Someone probably decided to get revenge on him."

Go, Murphy, I told him in thought.

Murphy yawned, then flew off whilst Ash and Tye's attention was focused on their screens.

I had to get my hands on those samples.

Ash got up and motioned for me to follow him. Damn, where were we going?

We headed over into another room that looked like a testing lab. All stainless steel and strange looking bits of equipment. Ash grabbed Murphy before he had a chance to get near the sample.

He took hold of my arm and led me into an empty office while keeping hold of Murphy. "Please tell me you're not trying to steal samples." Ash rubbed his forehead.

"Okay, I'm not."

"Cassie." He scowled and blew out a breath. "I know you better than anyone."

I knew better than to deny it. "Technically, Murphy was gonna take it." I lifted my dragon away from him.

"We're partners, but I'm still an enforcer. There are rules. You can't just go off and do whatever you want."

"A good investigator uses all the resources at their disposal." My mum had always taught me that. Even though she was a stickler for the rules. Just like Ash.

"Ivy has a record. I can't work with her."

"I'm a private investigator. Which means I *can* work with her," Cassie pointed out.

"Not on this you can't since you're a witness and could be considered a suspect."

"You know I'd never kill anyone. Not unless they were a monster."

"Yeah, but —"

"Come on. This is your first big case. Let me help you. Ivy could run tests on the down low. If she doesn't find anything, what do you have to lose?"

"I need to play by the rules on this one. I'm sorry."

"Fine. I better go." I turned to leave.

"I can't come patrolling tonight."

My mouth fell open. "What?"

"I have to work on the case. It wouldn't kill you to take a night off."

She shook her head. "I can't miss patrolling. Not when the Nether is more active than ever."

"You've patrolled a lot lately. Take a break. You know the rules. You're not supposed to slay things unless your magus is there with you. You could always call Cal to come and help you."

I scoffed. As if that would ever happen. "See you later."

CHAPTER 5

CASSIE

I headed to my advanced magic class the next morning. As much as I wanted to concentrate on the case I had to focus on classes or I'd be forced to catch up again like last term.

Lucy and Ivy trailed behind me as we headed out to the magical arts tower. This tower was smaller than some of the other ones. All sandstone and diamond-paned windows.

"I'm surprised you decided to take this class," Ivy told me. "We thought you'd be busy with the case."

"I still have to do classes. Besides, Ash won't let me officially help on the case."

"But you're doing it anyway." Lucy scoffed. "Ash won't let me help either. We helped last term. Why can't we help now? It's not like I'll go blabbing about the case to other people."

We took our seats at one of the wooden tables when we got to our class. The castle's grey stone walls were plastered with alchemical charts and other magical basics. Including slogans like: "magic is all about desire." And, "harm none do what thee will".

I almost rolled my eyes at the second one. Magic could always harm in some way. Just because there were laws against it didn't mean people wouldn't use magic to harm others. Look at Smiley — or Vikram rather. My mind raced with questions over his death. Who killed him? How had they killed him and why?

"Welcome, class. I'm Professor Ida Meriwether." An elf woman with long grey hair, pale skin and blue eyes took her place at the front of the class. "Now I'm not here to beat around the bush. I don't have the patience for time wasters. If you can't put in the work, you can leave my classroom right now."

This class didn't have as many annoying people as some of my other classes. No one moved to my surprise. At least the professor seemed no nonsense.

"Good, now let's get to work." Meriwether waved her hand and crystals appeared on the tables in front of everyone. They were round, almost opaque crystals.

Oh no, was she going to test our magic? One professor had done that last term and it had been a disaster. My magic had been all over the place back then. I had it under control now, but I didn't want to test it again. I already knew what I excelled at and what I didn't. And I had all my classes picked out for this year.

"Today we are going to be practising the art of divination." A collective groan went through the room. "Mock it all you like, but all supernaturals have the ability to use divination tools. Today we're going to be testing using several different tools."

I almost groaned. I half hoped we would be learning more advanced magic. Sure, divination could be good. My gran was a seer and swore by it. Even though she had pretty reliable visions she still insisted on using various tools to help her.

I had visions, but they'd always been unreliable. Gran tried teaching me things like tarot cards, scrying and other stuff. I'd never had much luck with them. To me, the answers they gave were too vague to ever be useful.

"We'll start with a good old-fashioned crystal ball," Meriwether went on. "I want you all to focus on the crystal in front of you.

Then I'll go around and ask you what you see."

I sighed. This wasn't what I needed to be doing. I should have been helping Ash, not messing around with crystals.

No. I said I'd be more focused on school stuff this term. I planned to stick to that. No matter what. No matter how useless some of the classes might seem.

"This is so boring." Ivy groaned. "We're supposed to be learning magic. Staring into crystals is something hack fortune tellers do."

"Shush," Lucy hissed. "Divination is one of the most ancient forms of magic. Treat it with respect."

"And one of the most unreliable." Ivy shook her head. "Magic and learning should be about proven methods. Humans trick people with crystals every day."

"Chill and stare at the crystal," Lucy snapped at her.

I kept my attention on my crystal. I should have sat with someone else. Lucy and Ivy always bickered no matter what we did together.

A whooshing sound shot towards me, then Murphy crash landed on the table with a diamond necklace clutched in his mouth.

"Oh, crap!" I gasped and energy pulsed

through my hands.

The class became motionless except for me and my roommates.

"Goddess, what have you done?" Lucy gaped at me. "You can't freeze the class! Someone could walk in and notice. Hell, the professor will probably notice when she unfreezes again."

"Forget that. Murphy, where the heck did you get these?" I grabbed hold of the necklace.

"Where did he get that? Are they diamonds?" Ivy asked. "Careful you don't break that."

I turned to the necklace but Murphy refused to let go of it. "Murphy, let go. Diamonds bad."

Murphy growled.

"How does he have that?" Lucy glanced around. "Cass, you can't keep the class frozen. You could get us all into trouble."

"You can't exactly let the professor see your dragon with diamonds either," Ivy pointed out. "Where did he get them?"

"He gets bored. He's getting more adventurous." I tugged again. "Murphy, drop."

"Pretty sure none of us have diamonds. Or are they a new slayer accessory?"

I scoffed. "Slayers have no use for diamonds. Murphy!" Murphy gripped the necklace tighter.

"Murphy, let go," Ivy urged.

"He's an adolescent dragon. I read they get more possessive at this stage," Lucy said. "You need to be firmer with him."

"Murphy, drop it!" I demanded. He just growled and flew into the air. "Murphy! Someone grab him."

Lucy flapped her wings and shot into the air. She made a grab for him but missed.

"I have an idea." Ivy picked up her backpack and rummaged through it. She pulled out a spray bottle, rose into the air and squirted it at Murphy. "Drop that right now."

Murphy wailed and the necklace clattered onto the table.

Lucy grabbed the necklace as she landed. "Whoa, I think these are real."

"Murph, where did you get these?" I demanded. "You know you're not supposed to steal things."

"Oh, shit." Lucy gasped.

"What now?" Ivy landed next to me, spray bottle still in hand.

"These diamonds have the mark of the royal elven family on them. I think these are Elora's."

"You've gotta be joking. Where would he get these? Elora might be a diva, but she doesn't parade around campus in her diamonds."

"It doesn't matter. We'd better get them back to her room before she notices they're gone." Lucy shoved the necklace in her bag. "We'll take them back after class. I know where her room is."

"How can you get in there?" My heart raced. I couldn't believe Murphy had gotten us into this mess.

Maybe he'd been restless and returned to the academy. Damn, I should have taken him on patrol with me. He seemed happy in the forest last year. Maybe it was because of his adolescent stage.

The room unfroze and noise returned. To my relief, Murphy flew off again. But he didn't seem happy at losing the diamonds. I just hoped he wouldn't steal anything else. I didn't have time to go around fixing his mistakes.

My mind raced so I turned my attention back to the crystal ball.

Professor Meriwether came over to our table. "What do you girls see?" She wanted to know.

Lucy narrowed her eyes. "All I see is

shadows."

Ivy sighed. "All I see is the crystal. I don't see anything else. Staring into crystals is useless anyway."

The professor frowned. "You must learn to see with your third eye, Miss Blue. Not everything about magic comes down to scientific explanation. Try again."

I turned my attention back to my crystal. I never had much luck with these. Taking a few deep breaths to clear my racing thoughts, I focused on it. Trying not to let thoughts of Murphy's antics bother me.

True, we could all get into serious trouble if Elora found out Murphy had taken her diamonds. It wasn't as if I'd asked him to take them. But that wouldn't matter to her.

My crystal blurred over and light flashed through it. I reached out to touch it. Energy jolted through me as a vision dragged me in.

Shadows surrounded the alleyway as someone knelt by Vikram's body and glanced back at me.

Liv.

I gasped as my vision faded. What the hell? Why would I see Liv?

She was gone. There was no reason why I'd see her.

"What did you see?" Meriwether gave me a

knowing look.

"Nothing." I didn't know what to tell her. It was probably better not talking about my sister. If anyone ever heard about this, it'd bring on the jeering and accusations again.

"You had a vision. Though I'd suggest not touching the crystal to get one. You're supposed to channel your energy through it."

"I…" I hesitated. Should I tell her? "I think I saw my sister." I kept my voice low to avoid anyone else hearing me.

"Wow," Lucy muttered under her breath and Ivy shook her head.

Meriwether nodded. "What else?"

"Just…shadows. It was just a flash. I've never been good with visions. They're too unpredictable to be useful to me."

"Shadows can mean many things. Perhaps something is hidden. Yet to be revealed," she said. "Given who your gran is, you should work on honing your gift more."

"My what? You know my gran?"

"Everyone knows of the McGregor witch. Focus on honing your gift. I sense you have untapped potential."

"Damn, I can't believe I'm bad at divination," Lucy grumbled as we left the class. "The one thing I was really looking forward to this year."

"Wow, you're bad at something. Big deal." Ivy rolled her eyes and hooked her backpack over her shoulder. "I told you divination is a waste of time."

"Then why are you taking it?" Lucy raised her eyebrows.

"Because it's another required class." Ivy sighed.

"At least you saw something." Lucy turned her attention to me. "Did you really see Liv?"

I nodded. "Yeah. No idea what it means. Let's just get to Elora's room before our next class."

"Good luck." Ivy turned to leave.

"Where are you going?" Lucy frowned at her.

"I'm not breaking into the princess's room. Having one criminal record is bad enough."

"Ivy, you're the only one who can help get us in there. We have less than thirty minutes." I glanced at my watch as we headed towards the housing block.

"What? No, it's your dragon. Your problem." Ivy scowled at me.

"Do you want her to get expelled?" Lucy demanded. "Remember what she did for you last term? You never would have got to —"

"Okay!" Ivy huffed out a breath. "Goddess,

if you get me expelled, Grey, I'll blow you up." She glowered at Lucy.

"Come on, there will be security on the room. Ivy, you need to make us invisible," I told her. "We need to move fast."

"How did your damn dragon get in there?" Ivy asked.

"I don't know. He has a way of getting into places." Ivy took hold of my hand then Lucy's and light flashed around us as we became invisible.

We took the lift to the twelfth floor. This was a private lift with a huge mirror on the back wall and a plush red carpet on the floor. It even had a red velvet seat for people to sit on. Of course Elora had a penthouse with its own private way of getting in. I was amazed she didn't have an entire housing block to herself.

"Oh, shit." I cursed when I spotted the alarm system on the door.

"That's a matrix system." Ivy gasped. "That's one of the best around. I'll never get through that."

She had a point. I knew how security systems worked but there'd be no getting through this one.

"Damn it. How else will we put them back?" Lucy asked.

My mind raced.

Murphy? Murphy, come to me. Right now.

Nothing.

Murphy!

"He's not answering my calls."

Lucy shrugged. "Maybe he's sulking because you scolded him and took the diamonds away."

"Luce!"

"What? He's a teenager. Teens sulk no matter what species they are. You'll have to lure him back."

Murphy, get here right now.

Still nothing.

"Murphy, Cassie's in danger," Lucy called out. "You don't want her to get hurt, do you?"

"Really?" Ivy put her hand on her hip and scoffed. "You think that's going to work on him?"

"We've got to try everything." Lucy shrugged. "Murphy, come here. There's a good boy." Her voice sounded gentler this time.

To my surprise, Murphy appeared in a flash of light and flew over to her. Typical. He'd probably be in a complete strop with me all day.

"Maybe you just need to be nicer to him."

Lucy patted Murphy's head.

I gritted my teeth and had to bite back a retort. It was his fault we were in this mess to begin with. "Murphy, come here." I tried to keep my voice gentle, but he could probably hear the edge in it.

Murphy ignored me and perched on Lucy's shoulder.

Traitor.

"Murphy, come here," I demanded again.

Still he ignored me.

"Will you stop encouraging him?" I glowered at Lucy as she continued to pet him.

"I can't help it. When he flashes those big eyes at me it's hard not to fall for him."

Ivy rummaged in her bag again and held up the spray bottle. "I have this and I will use it on you again unless you do as you're told."

Murphy hissed at her and reluctantly flew over to me.

"Took you long enough. Murph, I need you to be a good boy and transport us inside that room." I motioned towards the door and took hold of Lucy and Ivy again. "Can you do that?"

Murphy wrapped himself around my shoulders and blue light flashed around us.

We reappeared in a room with bright pink walls and a plush cream carpet. All of the furniture was a mix of white and pink. So sickly sweet it almost made my teeth hurt.

"Good boy." I patted Murphy's head, but he flew away from me. "You really need to stop sulking, boy. You know what you did was wrong. If you take people's things again, I could end up in big trouble. Heck, you might not even be allowed to live with me anymore."

Murphy growled and flew all around the room, investigating other items.

"Wow, all of this stuff must cost a fortune," Lucy breathed.

"I'd be able to do whatever I wanted if I had this level of wealth," Ivy remarked. "Guess that's a perk of being a princess. Although all of this pink looks rather tacky."

"Never mind that. Murphy, show me where you got these diamonds from." I held up the necklace but Murphy ignored me.

Ivy held at the spray bottle again. "I will use this," she threatened.

Murphy hissed then flew off towards another door. I followed after him. "Look around and see if there's anything that could hold jewellery."

I opened the door to reveal a much larger room with an enormous pink canopied fourposter bed. Murphy flew over to a large white vanity table. Bottles of perfume and pallets of makeup were scattered everywhere. They looked as if they'd been knocked over.

"Shit, Murphy, did you make all this mess?" I groaned. "She's gonna know someone was here." I opened my backpack and rummaged around until I found a can of Seal-It. A spray used by enforcers to make sure they didn't disturb evidence at crime scenes. I sprayed my hands so I wouldn't leave any fingerprints. I quickly rearranged the bottles as best I could and looked around for any sign of where the diamonds had come from. "Where did you get this?" I asked again and held up the necklace.

Murphy inclined his head towards a red velvet box etched with gold leaf that stood half open. I shoved the diamonds inside and closed the box.

"Murphy, listen to me. You can never come here again. If you do, I'll do worse than giving you a bath. Okay?" Murphy huffed and I only hoped this was the last of his thieving ways.

I turned to leave when Murphy flew over to the bedside table and grabbed a silver photo frame.

"Goddess, did you listen to anything I just said?" I stomped over to him and grabbed the frame. The picture caught my attention. It was a photo of Vikram and Elora with their arms around each other.

Holy crap, was the eleven princess really involved with him? If so, this took Ash's case to a whole new level.

After we left the penthouse, I took out my phone to call Ash.

"Hey, I think I've got a new lead on the case. I —" I began when he picked up.

"Cass, you know you're not supposed to be investigating the case." I could hear the sigh in his voice.

"But I have a lead. Smiley — I mean Vikram —"

"Just focus on classes and slaying this term. You don't need to be involved this," Ash cut me off. "By the way, we need to cut back on patrols. I'll be too busy working on the case. I'll talk to you later." He hung up before I had a chance to say another word.

CHAPTER 6

ASH

I rubbed my temples and gulped down some foul-tasting coffee as I leaned back in my desk chair. Fatigue weighed me down as I glanced over at the overcast sky outside the tower's window. It had been over a week since Vikram's murder, and I was still no closer to getting any answers.

The noise of people murmuring and working at their desks droned around me. The office wasn't much to look at with whitewashed walls and signs and posters everywhere. The smell of burnt coffee never seemed to leave the place.

There were a lot of people who didn't like him, but most of them that I'd talked to so far had alibis. They had either been signing up at the main office for schedules or been in their dorm rooms.

"Hey, all the tests are back," Tye said as he came over my desk. "I'll have to rule the cause of death as undetermined."

"Some type of magic killed him." I picked my mug up again but realised it was empty.

"Yeah, but I can't identify what. It's something different. Probably from the Nether. That's all I've got."

I shook my head. "I can't afford to not close this case. Vikram's family is demanding to have his body released."

"Unless you can get me some samples to compare this to, I'm gonna have to close this case. I can't stall for much longer, mate." Tye walked off.

A scraping sound made me look down. A dragon tail peeked out of my desk drawer.

Murphy.

"Hey, what are you doing?" I reached down and pulled him out by his tail. Looked like he'd gorged all of the chicken cat treats that I kept in there. "Where's Cass?"

Murphy huffed and glanced back at the drawer.

"No, I don't have any more. Nor are you getting more any time soon. Stealing is bad, Murph. You're not getting more treats unless you stop stealing."

"Any updates?" Cal came over to my desk. "What's the dragon doing here?"

"He just came for a visit." I patted Murphy's head. "And no, I don't."

Cal blew out a breath. "Then I'll just have the case ruled —"

"Just give me a couple more days."

"Ash, you have nothing. You look exhausted. Is Cassie on patrol tonight?"

I hesitated. Cassie and I hadn't talked much over the last couple of days. I'd been so focused on the case I'd almost forgotten about patrolling.

"I..."

"Has Cassie been patrolling on her own?" Cal narrowed his eyes. "Ash —"

"I don't think she's been patrolling." We both knew that wasn't true. Cass wouldn't give up patrolling if I wasn't around. Even though I asked her to hold off for a while.

"Get some rest and make sure Cassie isn't out on her own. If anything happens to her..." He shook his head. "Go home. That's an order. You have until Monday to present new evidence. If not, the case will be ruled an undetermined death."

Reluctantly, I left the tower and told Murphy to take me to Cassie. Cal was right. I never should have let her patrol alone. So I had to check on her.

We reappeared out near the island's southern boundary close to where the island bordered both Elfhame and the Nether Realm.

Yep, she was out slaying. A dark elf flew through the air as Cassie kicked him away from her.

"Hey!" Ivy threw a potion vial at the other Drow, and he slumped to the ground.

What in the Nether? What were Lucy and Ivy doing here?

The first Drow lunged for Cassie and made a grab for her again. She blocked his blow. She swung her sword and sliced his head off then knelt and stabbed the second.

"Nice work." Lucy sat and scribbled something in a notebook. "Cool stun potion, Ivy."

"Er, what are you doing?" I asked as I walked over to them.

"Oh, look, the useless magus has returned." Cassie rolled her eyes. "What does it look like we're doing?"

"You deserted her, so someone had to fill in," Lucy said. "I'm her unofficial magus. Ivy just needs test subjects. So it's a win-win for all of us."

"You're not trained," I began. "Being a magus isn't just watching the slayer and writing things down."

"I've read the magus guidebook from cover to cover. Besides, you've been ignoring her all week." Lucy threw me a glare.

"Wow, you look like crap," Cassie remarked as she came over to me.

"Do you realise how much trouble —"

"We're not going to tell anyone, and neither are you. Plus, you told me to stay out of your case, remember?" Cassie pointed out. "You can't expect me to sit around and do nothing when things are still coming out of the Nether." She motioned to the glowing green wall of energy that showed the island's protective boundary. It was supposed to keep people on the island safe.

"Hey, at least we're helping her," Ivy snapped. "We can't just let her risk her life by herself."

"And you're experimenting on dark elves? Do you realise how dangerous that is? A slayer is supposed to kill them, not experiment on them." I glanced between them and crossed my arms.

Yeah, I'd neglected my magus duties. That much I'd admit. But having civilians along during patrols went against every rule in the book. Cal would kill me if he heard about this.

"The academy won't approve my request to test on live specimens. There's no rule that says I can't experiment on Drow," Ivy stated.

"She's right." Lucy nodded. "It's surprising how little is actually known about dark elves. No one seems to want to study them. There is no real explanation as to why they even lost their souls either." She held out her hand and threw a fireball at the dead Drow. "I've got the clean-up problem handled too."

"Okay, enough." I raised my hands in surrender. "Cass, can we talk? Alone?"

"Sure, we're gonna head home."

"Yep, see you at the tower." Ivy threw another vial and she and Lucy vanished in a whirl of smoke.

"So it's okay when you want to talk? Yet when I want to talk to you, you're nowhere to be found." Cassie put her hands on her hips.

"I'm sorry, alright? I know I haven't been there for you. I've been so focused on the case. So I thought I'd come and see you so I can get an outside perspective."

"I thought I wasn't allowed to work on the case?" Cassie arched an eyebrow.

"Cal's managed to keep your name out of it. And I…"

"It's okay. I missed you too." She grinned

and grabbed my arm. "Let's go back to the tower."

I transported us to her room. The space had whitewashed walls, she had decorated them with twinkling lights and a few posters and family pictures. Some were of her sister, Liv. Bookcases filled with books, crystals and other knickknacks covered one side of the room. On the other stood her bed covered in blue linens and a large hammock hung next to the wall where Murphy slept.

"Want some coffee?" Cassie asked. She had a coffeemaker in her room but it didn't look like she used it much.

"No, I've had enough of that."

She headed into her bathroom.

I sat down on her bed. On the other side of the room was a large window seat with cushions on it and Murphy lay stretched out on it.

"Murph paid me a visit earlier at the enforcers tower."

"He didn't steal anything, did he?" Cassie groaned, and I heard her moving around the bathroom.

"He scoffed some treats. Cal says I have until Monday to find new evidence, or the case will be ruled undetermined."

"He only died a week ago." Cassie snorted.

"Enforcers have to work fast. I'll still working on it, but some people are pushing to have it closed and ruled as an accident."

"That's insane. We both know he was murdered."

"Agreed. But I can't prove it. Death by unknown magic doesn't give me anything. The chancellor wants everyone to believe it was an accident. Having a murder on the island is bad." I leaned back on the bed and yawned.

"You haven't proved what type of magic killed him?" Cassie came out wearing a black vest and shorts that she usually wore to bed.

"No."

"And you still won't let Ivy test anything?" Cassie came over and sat on the bed beside me.

"I guess we could try."

Her eyes widened. "What? Wow. Are you feeling alright? You must be sick or something." She touched my forehead. "Nope, I don't think you have a fever."

"Maybe I need to think outside the box."

"Ivy!" Cassie called and touched around a crystal on her bedside table. "Ash has agreed to let you run some tests on Smiley's case."

Cassie's door flew open. "Wow, are you

serious?" Ivy beamed as she rushed into the room.

"Yeah, as long as you're discreet." I lay back on Cassie's bed.

"I can do that. I'll need to see your case files and know what tests that idiot you work with has done so far."

I scowled. "Hey, Tye's not an idiot."

Ivy waved her hand in dismissal. "You're right. Forget I said that. When do we get started?"

"Geez, let the guy sleep. We'll do tests tomorrow," Cassie said.

Ivy's smile widened. "Great, Ash, can you send me over the cases file straightaway? I want to get dug in so I can get an idea of what's been done so far."

"I can't give you the case files." I shook my head. "No one gets to see those unless they have the correct clearance."

"How do you expect me to work then?" Ivy demanded.

"We'll go over things tomorrow. Go." Cassie motioned her away.

Ivy went to the door and hesitated. "If you have sex, can you please keep the noise down?"

"What?" I gaped at Ivy. "We're not —"

"What you two do is your business. See

you in the morning." Ivy closed the door behind her as she left.

"Exactly how many guys do you bring back here?" I grinned at Cassie.

"You're the only one so don't get too excited." She thumped my shoulder. "You missed me, didn't you?"

"Maybe. Still don't see why you needed to move out."

"Because this place is bigger. And I'm not sure you'd like living here with two other women."

"I should go." I yawned but didn't make a move to get up. My eyelids grew heavy.

"Whatever." Cassie snuggled against me and rested her head on my chest.

Eventually, we both fell asleep, and I couldn't help but think how nice it was just to be close to her again.

Hot, smelly breath woke me up as sunlight streamed in through Cassie's balcony doors. I almost jumped when I found Murphy nose to nose with me.

"What in the Nether?" I groaned. "Murphy, what are you doing?"

Cassie lay snuggled against me. Her head on my shoulder as she held onto me.

Crap, I couldn't believe I'd fallen asleep in

her bed. How could I be so stupid? Yeah, I'd been exhausted but there were lines I couldn't cross. This was one of them.

"Cass, I think your dragon wants feeding." I shoved Murphy off me.

Murphy chirped and flew into the air. He hovered above the bed.

"Ash?" someone called my name and the front door banged open.

Oh shit. That sounded like Cal. Why in the Nether was he here? How did he know I was here?

Murphy landed on my chest again.

"Murphy, get off me!" I pushed, but he refused to move. A few moments later the door was flung open. Cal came in followed by Nina Morgan, Cassie's aunt and adoptive mother, who looked shocked.

Cal glowered at me. "What in the Nether are you two doing?"

Cassie jolted awake. "What the fuck are you doing in my room?" she demanded and glowered back at him.

"I'm asking the same thing. You know it's forbidden —"

"Cal, we didn't do anything. I just fell asleep here." I motioned to my clothes and shoes which were still attached to my body.

"You two shouldn't be sharing a bed," Cal

snapped. "You —"

"Alright, how about we all calm down?" Nina interjected. She ran a hand through her long lilac coloured hair and her blue eyes flicked between each of us.

"We wouldn't exactly be having sex with my dragon in bed with us, would we?" Cassie rolled her eyes. "Now why the hell are you both here?"

"We came to talk to you about something, but I see now isn't a good time." Nina shook her head.

I slid off the bed. "We haven't done anything wrong. I —" I knew Cal would be furious. He'd always warned me not to get romantically involved with Cassie.

"Look, we fell asleep. Nothing has happened. Get out of my room." Cassie continued to glare at Cal.

"You know the rules —" Cal began.

"You didn't care about the rules when you slept with my mother and left her to die, did you?" Cassie demanded. Cal's anger faded and all the colour drained from his face. "So fuck you, Cal, and forget about this. Ash isn't stupid enough to break your precious rules."

"Alright, that's enough." Nina stepped forward. "They're fully clothed for goodness sake. Cassie, we need to talk. We'll wait for you downstairs." Nina grabbed Cal's arm and dragged him out.

"Shit, I'm sorry." I ran a hand through my tousled hair.

"Don't be. You've got nothing to feel guilty about. All we did was sleep."

"I left you on your —"

"I was fine, and he doesn't need to know that. How did he know you were here?" Cassie scowled.

"That's a good question. Why is Nina here?"

Cal could have been looking for me. But Nina? I couldn't understand why she and Cal would be together.

"No idea!" Cassie muttered the elven word for clean to give herself a quick magical shower then headed to the bathroom. "Guess we'll find out."

"I'll deal with Cal. Later we'll go and get the testing done."

I headed downstairs and found Nina in the kitchen making some coffee.

"Cal's outside waiting for you," she told me.

"Nothing happened between us."

Nina scowled at me. "Make sure it doesn't. I already lost my sister; I won't lose Cassie too."

"I'd never let —"

"You can't always be there for her, can you? It doesn't sound like you've been around much lately."

"What do you mean?"

"You can't be a magus and an enforcer. It doesn't work like that. And I see the way you look at Cassie. No good will come from that. Cal is right."

"I… Nothing's happened."

"But it could, and probably will, happen. I won't watch her die. The goddess knows I never wanted her to be a slayer. If you care about her, do the right thing."

I had no idea what she meant. What did she consider to be the right thing? The right thing to me was being Cassie's magus. Sure, we'd had a few problems since the case. But that might be over in a couple of days.

Nothing had happened. Sleeping next to each other wasn't crossing the line. I'd never cross that line. Not even if I wanted to.

Cal sat on a bench outside. "I expected better from you."

"For fuck's sake. Nothing happened," I snapped. I rarely got angry with him. He'd always been like a father to me, but he was still my boss.

"But it could have."

"It won't. You have my word on that."

"Are you saying you don't have feelings for her?"

"I — She's my best friend. Always has been. We understand each other in a way no one else can."

"I know how easy it is for lines to blur. Until they no longer matter," Cal said. "If you cross that line, one or both of you will end up dead."

"Good thing I'll never cross it. Now why are you here?"

Cal leaned back on the bench. "The elven queen has demanded I close Vikram's case."

"You promised me two days to find something else."

"And you have them. I suggest you hurry. I didn't just come here for you. Nina and I have come to talk to Cassie. Although I'm not sure I'll be welcomed back in."

A few moments later, Cassie stormed out of the tower, now fully dressed.

"Why are you still here?" She glared at her dad.

"I was just leaving." Cal vanished in a flash of light.

Cassie's shoulders sagged as some of the tension left her. "Want to stay for breakfast?

Mum already left."

"Okay."

Breakfast started in awkward silence. Maybe I should have left.

"So what's the plan for today?" Ivy came down and joined us in the kitchen.

Cassie hadn't said much. I didn't know if she was embarrassed or just didn't want to talk.

"We need to somehow get samples from the Nether," I stated. "That's not gonna be easy. The Nether is unpredictable and intangible."

"Can't be if everything keeps coming out of it," Ivy pointed out.

"I've called Tye. Maybe the two of you can —"

"No. I work alone." Ivy shook her head. "I can't deal with someone messing things up."

"Tye is damn good at what he does."

"Those are my terms. I work alone and no one interferes."

"You need me and Ash there," Cassie pointed out. "Being near the Nether is dangerous."

"I mean other than you two," Ivy said. "Lucy said she's gonna do research on the Nether in the library to see if she can find anything."

"Let's get going."

We reappeared near the border to the Nether Realm.

"Still can't believe no one has ever taken samples," Ivy remarked.

"Going near the Nether is pretty much forbidden unless you're a slayer or a magus," I said. "The chancellor will have a meltdown if she finds out about this."

"I know how to be careful." Ivy grinned. "I've dreamt of this."

"You dream of people being killed?" I frowned at her.

"No, I dream of testing things like this."

"This is Ivy in her element." Cassie rolled her eyes and took hold of my arm to lead me back a few steps.

Ivy ignored us and got to work, pulling out various pieces of equipment.

"Mum came to tell me I'm being summoned by the council again."

My frown deepened. "Why?"

She shrugged. "No idea. I have to be there tomorrow morning."

"I'll come with you."

"You said you had to work on the case."

"There won't be much for me to do if Ivy

can't get any samples."

Being summoned by the council usually never meant anything good. I didn't know why they'd want to summon Cassie. They already knew she was the slayer.

"I still can't believe Cal went off like that. It's not like anything ever happened between us. Not that it would." Her cheeks flushed. "I mean, don't get me wrong you're gorgeous but…"

"Right." I looked away. She was right. Nothing could ever happen between us. No matter how much I cared about her.

A blast of energy knocked Ivy off her feet. "Ow! Shit! It fried my scanner." Ivy groaned.

"And this is why we don't know much about the Nether." I chuckled.

Ivy tried several other devices and every time she tried something her equipment either exploded or melted.

"It's a good thing I brought old stuff with me," Ivy remarked. "Damn it, how can I get samples? Everything that touches the Nether gets destroyed."

"Let me try." Cassie stepped forward. "Maybe I can get some of the magic out and grab it."

"Make sure you hang onto this. It's supposed to be an unbreakable test tube. It should be able to hold any kind of magic no matter how volatile it is." Ivy handed her a glass vial.

Cassie reached out to the glowing barrier of energy.

Light flashed and Cassie vanished.

CHAPTER 7

CASSIE

I gasped as I stumbled into the Nether. Glowing green mist enveloped me. The air left my lungs in a whoosh. I couldn't see anything but the green hue.

"Cassie!" I thought I heard Ash, but his voice sounded far away.

"Cassie!" another voice called for me. "Cassie, hurry. Run upstairs and hide. Go! Now!"

What the hell?

Glass smashed and the sounds of screaming filled my ears.

Goddess, what was happening to me?

I clutched my ears. I had to get the hell out of here. But first I had to get something Ivy could use.

I reached out and tried to draw some of the

Nether's energy to me. Green light flashed around me then evaporated.

Nothing.

Smoke curled around my fingers and evaporated.

Gritting my teeth, I drew my light magic and caught hold of a few wisps in the bottle. Not much but it would have to do.

I shoved the vial into my jacket and pushed against the mist. A wall of resistance met me.

What the heck? If I could get into the Nether, then I could get out.

I pushed harder, but still, I couldn't pass back through.

Nothing.

Gritting my teeth harder, I called out, "Ash! Ash, I can't get back. Are you there?" In truth, I had no idea if he would hear me. I never expected to be pulled through into the Nether itself.

No response came. I couldn't hear him call for me either.

"Ash!"

Fine, I'd just have to find a way out by myself. I drew magic but it fizzled out.

"Magic doesn't work in the Nether," a voice rang through my ears.

"Who's there?" I called out but no one responded.

"Not in the Space Between."

The Space Between.

That seemed familiar. A place that existed between the Nether and the real world.

Damn, why hadn't I realised I'd get sucked in?

My birth mum warned me about that. Like me, she had been the slayer before she had been killed seven years ago. For a long time I had put all thoughts of being a slayer out of my mind. At least up until last year when I realised I couldn't ignore my slayer heritage any longer. Right around the time I'd found Murphy, and Ash had come back into my life.

Strange. I thought I'd forgotten a lot of things she'd taught me. Maybe some of them were coming back.

"Run, Cassie!" a voice screamed at me again.

I reached for my sword and realised I had laid it on the grass back in the field in front of the boundary.

Bugger!

The screaming intensified and things crashing to the ground echoed around me.

Where did all that noise come from? What the hell was it?

It couldn't be from the Nether, could it? Well, no one really knew how the Nether worked. Maybe it was another memory. I knew I couldn't stay here. People who went into the Nether never came out again. That was one thing all slayers, elves and other supernaturals were warned about.

People who'd gone through were never seen again. Estelle had ingrained that in me for as long as I could remember.

Think, there has to be a way out of here.

Nothing came to mind. So much for that helpful voice I'd heard earlier.

Is there anyone there? I called out in thought. *Can you help me out of here?*

No reply came. Maybe that voice had been a memory too. But from where? It sounded familiar yet I couldn't place it.

I pushed further against the barrier. This time in the opposite direction. The Space Between was more than just mist. Or at least I thought it was.

Stumbling, I appeared in what looked to be woods. The trees blurred in and out of existence. Their elongated branches reaching for me like searching arms, waiting to grab me and drag me deeper into the depths of the Nether.

Something told me not to go too far. If I went into the Nether Realm itself, I had no idea what I'd face. Other than no chance of getting home again. And to think being found in bed with Ash and a summons from the council had been my only problems this morning.

"Murphy?" I called.

Murphy could travel in and out of other realms. If anyone could help get me out of this nightmare, it'd be him.

Come on, Murphy. I need you.

Nothing.

Murphy! Come here. I need help.

My dragon didn't appear. Guess I'd have to find my own way out. I doubted my powers would be any good here.

I kept on walking. The trees continued flashing in and out, still reaching for me, so I made sure to give them a wide berth. Would I even know if I ended up in the Nether? Would I cease to exist or be trapped in some kind of hell for the rest of eternity?

As I walked, I thought back to my conversation with Mum earlier.

"Why've you come here with Cal?" I asked her.

Mum blew out a breath. "Because the elven council has summoned you. The letter was sent to our house rather than here." She placed an envelope with a wax seal on the kitchen table.

"Why?" I picked it up and ripped it open.

All it said was Cassandra Morgan, the elven council request your presence tomorrow morning at a meeting room on the main campus. Attendance of this meeting is mandatory and if you do not attend enforcers will be sent to collect you.

That sounded just like the council. Abide by their rules or there would be hell to pay.

"That's it? What do they want?"

Mum shrugged. "I don't know. I'll come and —"

"You don't need to be there." I shook my head.

"Nothing good ever comes from the elves. Your gran will be there too. So it must be important."

I still couldn't imagine what the council had to say to me. Nor would I worry about it.

The trees seemed to blur together. Maybe I was going the wrong way. I turned around. The path I'd been on had vanished.

Great. Just bloody great. Was this the Space Between or the Nether Realm?

I stumbled and felt my limbs grow heavy. I had to keep moving. I couldn't stay here.

"Move. Move through the Space Between. Nothing can stay there. It's a barrier between this world..." that voice echoed around me again.

I caught a flash of a room with lilac walls. Weird. It seemed familiar somehow, but I couldn't quite place it.

"Murphy!" I called for him again.

I had to keep moving. If I stayed here much longer, I'd be trapped forever. Then I'd be one of the Nether Realm's forgotten victims.

After that, I'd be dead or worse, stuck here forever in Limbo. Alone and reliving the nightmare over and over again.

My head spun and my vision blurred. Bile rose in my throat and I swallowed it down again.

I'm not gonna die here.

The darkness intensified so much it became hard to see anything. There had to be a way out of here somewhere. This was the Space Between.

"The Space Between exists before the Nether. A boundary to stop people from getting lost between the realms…" that voice came again.

My eyes blurred and the shadows swallowed me up. I raised my hand to conjure an orb of light.

Nothing. Only darkness existed here, and I became part of it.

I groaned as I opened my eyes. Light and darkness blurred together.

"Easy now, girl," a gruff voice said.

My senses went on alert as I shot up. The room whirled around me. I coughed as I spewed my guts up.

"I said take it easy. Typical slayer." The gruff voice sighed. "You need to rest. Shadow sickness is nasty stuff. Even for you."

I turned towards the voice. It took a few moments for a face to swim into focus. An old crone with one beady eye and straggly grey hair stared back at me. Vinessa. A seer I met last year.

"Welcome back to the land of the living, slayer." She passed me a large wooden bowl. "You'll need this."

"What..." I threw up again. "What's wrong with me?"

"It's Shadow Sickness. It comes from the Space Between."

I rested the bowl on my knees. "How did..." I groaned as my stomach lurched again.

Vinessa shoved a cup towards me. "Drink this."

Thinking it was water I gulped it down. "Christ, what is this? It's like swamp —"

"A potion to remove the last of the sickness."

I groaned, shoved the bowl aside and put my head between my knees. "How'd I get here?"

"Heard the trees whispering. You were close to getting out of the Space Between, but the sickness got the better of you before you had a chance. If I hadn't found you, you would've been trapped there. You should know better than to go there, slayer."

"It wasn't my choice. I got sucked through the boundary."

"What were you doing so close to it?"

"Trying to get some samples of Nether magic."

Vinessa laughed, a harsh gravelly sound. "No one can catch Nether magic. Why would you do something so stupid?"

I hesitated and pushed my damp hair off my face. Hopefully I'd stop vomiting now. Should I tell her anything? I only met her once, but I knew Ash came to see her for advice sometimes.

Vinessa's advice always came with a price, though.

"Someone on the academy island was killed. We think something came out of the Nether," I admitted.

Vinessa snorted. "Bet the chancellor don't like that, does she?"

"The Elhanan wants the death to be ruled as accidental. I'm not convinced it was an accident." I pushed the bowl of vomit further away. "Why did you save me? Are you expecting me to pay a price for it?"

"You're too valuable to all supernaturals, slayer. Not just us elves." Vinessa rose and headed over to the bubbling cauldron on the hearth.

I fell silent and stood up. My legs gave out from under me, and I hit the floor.

"I told you to rest." Vinessa shook her head. "You're like your mother."

I grabbed onto the side of the bed and yanked myself up. "You mean Estelle."

"Of course. She's your mama, ain't she? She taught you what it means to be a slayer."

I slumped back on the bed. My mind raced with questions. Should I ask Vinessa about Vikram's murder? My thoughts drifted back to the voice I'd heard in the Space Between. Who had that been?

"Is it normal to hear voices in the Space Between?"

"The Space Between affects people in different ways. What did you see or hear?"

Again, I hesitated but didn't see the harm

in telling her. "Someone spoke to me. Told me it was the Space Between. Then I kept hearing someone screaming."

"What else did they say?"

"They told me to run. No idea why. Nothing chased or attacked me."

"Did you recognise the voice?"

Pondering the question, I bit my lip. "It sounded familiar. No idea who it was, though. The voice told me about the Space Between and what it could do. That's how I knew I had to get out. Could someone have been warning me?" Somehow, I doubted anyone in the Nether would want to help me.

"Your memories are cloaked. It's possible you remembered something. Your mum would have taught you about the Space Between."

"Estelle? Wait, why would someone cloak my memories of her? That doesn't make any sense. I remember what she taught me about being a slayer."

"Some yes, but not all of it. Maybe it's coming back to you. Maybe she cloaked your memories until you are ready to remember them."

"Is someone killing people on the island? What do you know?" I sat up and arched an eyebrow at her.

"That will cost you."

No surprise there.

I waved a hand in dismissal. "Name your price."

Vinessa shook a crooked finger at me. "Careful, slayer. My prices are steep for a reason."

"Name it, then I'll decide if I wanna pay it."

"I want a favour from you."

"What kind of favour?" I furrowed my brow.

"That's for me to decide."

"Fine, tell me what you know."

Vinessa's wrinkled lips twisted into a smirk. "That man's death wasn't natural."

"And?" I persisted.

"Something is there. Someone is watching you. The answers you need will come in time. More have to die before you find the one in the shadows."

"That doesn't —"

"You wanted an answer, slayer. I gave you one. That's all you get."

"Fine." I got to my feet, unsteady. "How do I get out of here?" My legs almost gave way again.

"He'll take you back to the academy."

"Who?"

The front door flew open, and Ash rushed

in.

"Goddess, where've you been? I thought..." He wrapped his arms around me.

"Hi." I hugged him back. "I...got a little lost in the Space Between."

"The what?" Ash gaped at me.

"The Space Between the Nether and this realm." I looked at him like it was obvious.

"Cass, I've got no idea what you're on about. There is no Space Between the Nether and this realm."

I glanced over at Vinessa, but she was too focused on her cauldron to pay any attention to me.

"Tell him," I urged.

"He's stuck in the old ways, slayer."

"There's a space, like Limbo before you reach the Nether," I explained. "That's where I went."

"But no one comes out of the Nether."

"The Space Between is different from the Nether, boy." Vinessa shook her head. "Maybe you could learn a thing or two from your slayer."

"Let's go. Come on, Cass."

"She needs rest. She had Shadow Sickness," Vinessa called after us, as Ash led me out of the dilapidated cottage.

"Can you tell me what happened?" Ash

asked. "I thought I'd lost you."

As we headed back to the transfer stone, I filled him in on what happened.

"Wait, you think you remembered Estelle telling you about the Space Between?" Ash frowned.

"Yeah. Maybe. Everything was messed up in there."

"Cal always said Estelle wasn't like most slayers. She didn't play by the rules."

"Whatever. Let's just get back to the island."

CHAPTER 8

ASH

My stomach did flip-flops the next morning as I stood outside the meeting hall on the academy's main campus. I'd offered to go with Cassie for moral support.

"Any idea what this might be about?" she asked me.

I shrugged. "Could be anything."

I'd asked Cal what he knew about today's meeting, but he refused to say. I didn't see the need for secrecy either. Cal was the only one with real connections with the council so I couldn't get any more answers.

"It can't be because I am the —"

Don't mention the S word around here. I switched to speaking in thought. *And no, they already know what you are.*

"Maybe it's about the case," Cassie suggested.

"Doubt it. They wouldn't summon you for that." My mind raced as Cassie paced up and down. "We're early. The council never gets here before the scheduled time."

"I want to get this over with." Cassie looked different in her dress and shoes rather than her usual jeans and boots.

"Just relax." I put a hand on her shoulder.

"Relax? I could be imprisoned or worse because the damn council decides they don't like having me around."

"Don't be daft. They need you. We all do." I glanced around. "You didn't bring Murphy."

"No. I don't want him near them. Besides, he's too unpredictable right now in his teenage phase."

"Maybe we should go for a walk."

"What does it look like I'm doing?" Her heels clanked against the marble floor as she continued pacing.

"Come on." I grabbed her hand and pulled her down the hall. We headed down the corridor.

"I wonder if Elora is back at the academy? She hasn't been around much the last few days."

I arched a brow. "Why?" From what I'd seen so far Cassie and the elven princess didn't get along very well.

We headed up to the next floor. I knew the academy well enough to know there was a balcony that overlooked the meeting room.

"I'm surprised the elven council are coming here," I remarked. "Usually they only meet at the queen's palace."

"It must be bad if they're coming here," Cassie mused.

"Calm down. You can't let them see you're nervous."

"I'm not nervous." Purple light flared between her fingers.

"Your magic says otherwise."

"Ash!"

"Just relax. No matter what happens I'll be right there with you." I gripped her shoulders. "We're partners and I'll be right there with you."

She blew out a breath and turned her attention to the hall below us. "Wait, there's more than five seats at the head of the table. Who else is gonna be here?"

"Maybe the elven queen or perhaps they're seats for us."

"Doubt it. I've been to enough meetings with elves to know how they work."

"This is more than just the council. Maybe it's about the case."

"If it was, why wouldn't they summon you instead of me? Goddess, they don't think I had anything to do with the victim's death, do they?" She bit her lip.

My phone buzzed and I pulled it out to see it was a call from a number I didn't recognise. I frowned. "Hello?"

"Ash, is that you?"

"Yeah, who's this?"

The voice sounded female, but I couldn't place it.

"It's Princess Elora. I need to see you and your partner. That purple haired freak that you like to hang out with."

I gritted my teeth at her comment about Cassie. "What do you want, Elora?"

"I told you; I need to see you both. Right now."

"No can do. I have a meeting."

"I just gave you an order," she screeched. "Come to my apartment at once."

I winced at the sound of her voice. "You know I can't be late for a meeting with the council." I didn't want Elora to know about the meeting, so I didn't give her any details about it. No doubt the news would spread around the island like wildfire. I didn't have to say what it was about. Nor could I think of anything else to say.

"The council? Why are you being summoned?" She sounded confused.

"Don't know yet. But their summons can't be ignored. Have a good —"

"Please. I need to talk to you about Vikram," she pleaded. "You can't let them close his case."

My eyes widened. "Why would you care about Vikram's case? I thought you of all people would be happy to have it closed. You wouldn't want the academy to be seen in a bad light, would you?"

"She had a picture of him in her room," Cassie hissed. "Think they were involved."

"Please. You can't let them close it. Not without finding out what really happened to him." Elora sounded like she was sobbing.

My mouth fell open. "Okay, we can come and see you…" I glanced at my watch. We had half an hour before the council meeting.

"We'll come now," Cassie said.

"We don't have time." I shook my head.

"Yeah, we do. Let's go."

I sighed. "We'll be right there, but it'll have to be quick."

Cassie and I transported to the top level of the Magic Users Housing Block.

"Why didn't you tell me about Elora's possible involvement with Vikram?" I asked as we headed down the hall.

"Because you were ignoring me. Besides, I can't prove anything. Elora's friends won't talk to me, and she wasn't around for me to question. Come on, her room is this way. I've been there before."

We exited the lift and went down a red carpeted hallway with beige walls.

"How did you get in her room?"

"Long story involving Murphy and diamonds. You don't want to know." She shook her head. "Why did she ask to see me?"

I shrugged. "Just said she wanted to see both of us. We'll have to make this quick." I knocked on the door.

Elora opened the door a few moments later. An enormous elf in armour loomed behind the door.

"Come in." She motioned us in and for us to sit down on her plush cream sofa. "First I need you to sign these." She held out two clipboards to us.

I glanced down at my one. "It's an NDA." I furrowed my brow.

"Yes, you both need to sign them. I need to make sure nothing I tell you becomes public knowledge."

I shook my head. "You can trust us. There's no need for this."

"You must sign them," Elora snapped.

"As an enforcer, I can't." I put my clipboard down and shoved it away.

Elora turned to Cassie. "Then you —"

"I'm not signing either. Look, we know you were involved with Vikram, and Ash is the only one who can keep the case open. If you want our help, start talking," Cassie snapped.

Elora slumped back into the chair. "How could you know that? No one knew. We were discreet."

"Why did you call us?" I got straight to the point. We couldn't afford to waste time or we'd be late for the meeting.

"Because you have to keep the case open. You have to find out who killed him." Tears filled her eyes. "I know everyone hated him, but with me… He was different. He loved me."

"I can't keep the case open without any evidence," I pointed out. "Unless you make a statement and —"

"You know I can't. My mother would kill me if she found out I was involved with Vic."

"Tell us what you know," I went on. "Any enemies you both had. If anyone might know about your relationship."

Elora hesitated. "Sign —"

"You know that won't happen," Cassie said.

Elora sighed and went on to tell us she and Vikram had been involved for several months and gave us a list of potential enemies about a mile long.

"This isn't enough," I remarked.

Elora gaped at me. "I just gave you an entire list of new suspects."

"The chancellor wants the case closed. I need evidence to prove his death wasn't accidental. A list of names isn't enough."

"Why don't you just use your authority to keep the case open?" Cassie asked Elora. "Why ask us when you could do it yourself?"

Elora scoffed. "I can't. My power is limited."

"Your mother does," I pointed out. "If you went to her and asked her to keep it open, it'd give us more time to find out what happened to him."

Elora shook her head. "I can't. My mother never listens to anyone. She would laugh if I asked for this."

A knock came at the door and a few moments later, Tye rushed in.

"Here's the paperwork." He waved a piece of paper. Elora's guard made a grab for him.

"All we need is your signature," I told Elora. "One word from you and I will keep the case open."

Elora hesitated then grabbed the pen that Tye held out to her. "Fine. But I want to know every scrap of evidence you can find."

CHAPTER 9

CASSIE

Ash and I raced back to the castle. "Can't believe we just did that." Ash grinned, after we stopped running.

"Me either." Exhilaration rushed through me. "I can't believe she admitted it either. Unbelievable." I threw my arms around him. "See, we do make a good team. When you don't ignore me that is."

"I won't ignore you again." Ash brushed his lips against mine.

Shocked jolted through me and his eyes widened as if he realised what he had done.

"Shit," he muttered. "Cass, I'm—"

I cut him off with another kiss. Only this time he pulled away.

"Cass, we can't. I'm your magus and —"

"Cassie?" someone called out and Mum

strode down the hall.

My cheeks flushed. Damn, I hoped she hadn't seen that. I didn't even have time to think what the kiss might mean.

Instead, I plastered on a smile. "Mum, would you mind telling me what this is about?"

"Not sure yet. Good thing you're on time." Mum wrapped me in a hug. "Don't worry. We'll get this over with soon." Mum glanced over at Ash. "Surprised you're here. Haven't you got a case to solve?"

Ash reddened. "Er..."

"Mum, who's going to be at this meeting?" I cut in, not caring if Ash was embarrassed. I just wanted answers. Ash wouldn't even look at me now. Bastard. He kissed me first. I'd make sure we talked about this later.

Mum shrugged. "The council."

"And?" I knew she wasn't telling me the whole truth.

"Maybe some other people." Mum bit her lip.

"You know what it's about. Is it to do with Liv?"

"In part yes. For the past few months or should I say years, your mum and Liv's legacy statements have been in dispute between the McGregors, the fae and the elven courts."

All thoughts of the case and Ash shot out of my mind.

Legacy statements were like human wills. Most fae and elves wrote one to make sure any assets went to their chosen people. Next of kin didn't always apply depending on the person's wishes.

I'd never even thought much about Estelle's assets and what she had left us. I assumed Mum had taken them over. But Liv? I never thought she'd written a legacy statement. She was only twenty-five when she died. Liv did have assets. She had a successful music and modelling career before things quietened down over the last couple of years.

"Wait, why would the fae and elven courts care about Estelle and Liv's assets?"

"Because they both have a lot of money. Your mum was the slayer. No doubt they'd all like to get their hands on her knowledge." Mum grimaced. "Just be careful what you say in there. No doubt there will still be more arguing." She rolled her eyes.

We headed inside. Ash trailed after us.

"You don't have to stay," I told him.

His eyes widened. "I said I would."

"Don't you need to focus on the case? Now you have a way to keep it open?"

"No. I'll stay."

Fine, but we need to talk later, I added in thought.

Ash looked away and said nothing.

What I wouldn't give to know what was going on in his brain.

I pushed all thoughts of him away again. Damn him for confusing me at a time like this.

Mum and I took our seats and Ash sat behind us. After a while, Cal and members of the elven council came in. Followed by the elven queen herself.

Goddess, why would the queen bother herself with a legacy reading? I'd never met the queen before. She was beautiful. Blonde and willowy like her daughter. Her piercing blue eyes narrowed when she caught sight of me.

Can't say I'm happy to be here either.

I slumped back in my seat.

The doors opened. Silvana Eldry, the fae queen came in flanked by three fae guards. Silvy gave the elven queen a nod and a smile before taking her seat.

Geez, this felt weird. Why were my mother and sister's assets so valuable? Enough for fae and elven rulers to come here? Liv had money, that much I knew. But she never mentioned anything about property or other assets she might have.

One of the council leaders rose. "We are gathered here to discuss the legacy reading of Olivia Grace Morgan. Along with the assets of her mother, Estelle Morgan McGregor. Her assets have been held in trust until her daughters came of age."

"Bollocks. Olivia was already of age before she died," another voice snapped.

My gran, Magda McGregor, appeared in a flash of light. As the McGregor witch, she was pretty much royalty in the witch world. "And how dare you start without me," Gran added, sitting down between me and Mum.

"Your presence isn't required here," the elven queen sneered.

"Estelle and Olivia are my flesh and blood. Their legacies and assets are to go to my granddaughter, Cassie."

"Their assets are subject to my review," the elven queen snapped.

"May I remind you they were also fae? And under the jurisdiction of my court?" Silvy spoke up.

"Neither of you have any claim to my family's wealth, knowledge or power." Gran glowered at them.

"Estelle never left a legacy statement," the queen interjected. "Therefore any assets belong to me."

"That's not true. I have Estelle's legacy statement. Along with Olivia's." Cal rose to his feet and pulled out two sealed envelopes. "Estelle's instructions were not to read her statement until Cassie came of age. Olivia gave me this and her statement before she died."

"Why would Liv do that?" I demanded.

My gran glared at me, then turned her glare on Cal. "You have no right to either of those."

"That's why I called this meeting today." Cal stepped up to the dais. "Olivia and Estelle's statements are still sealed. Estelle's has never been opened. Only Cassie can open them and read them."

"Impossible," the elven queen snapped. "I —"

"Oh, do be quiet. Whoever writes the legacy can claim who reads it. That is true for all supernaturals." Cal came over and held the envelopes out to me.

"If you knew this, why was this meeting necessary?" Gran asked. "Why didn't you produce Estelle's statement before? It would have saved us years of arguing with the fae and elven courts."

"Because I abided by her wishes. Fae and elven law have to be followed. Hence, both monarchs being here."

"You shall open and read them to Tyron," the elven queen instructed me.

"I will not." I scowled at her. I couldn't believe she expected me to read out the contents of my family's legacy statements to a council leader let alone all the people here. Legacy statements were usually something read in private in front of family and chosen witnesses.

"Your sister is a murderer. Her assets are forfeit to —"

Gran held up her hand. "Not until the statements are read. So shut your mouth and let the girl read."

The elven queen turned red and sputtered.

I took the envelopes.

The first one read: *To my daughters, Liv and Cassie, only to be opened when you're of age.*

It felt odd seeing my birth mum's handwriting. The second read: *For my sister, Cassie Morgan.*

I opened Estelle's first. That seemed like the easier option. My sister's death was still too raw.

My eyes scanned over the words.

"Speak up then, girl," the elven queen snapped, which earned her another glare from Gran.

"I, Estelle Morgan McGregor, do hereby write my legacy statement. I, as elf slayer, hold claim to no court of fae, or elf. Hereby neither the fae, elf court or the clan McGregor shall have any claim to my lands, wealth, titles or properties." My eyes widened. I hadn't expected to read that. Estelle hadn't been stupid. She would have known what would happen if anything happened to her.

"Impossible —" the elven queen screeched.

"Be quiet," Silvy snapped. "You're not allowed to interrupt a reading."

"All my assets shall pass to my daughters, Olivia Grace McGregor and Cassie McGregor. They shall stay in the care of my sister until my daughters are of age. Should one of them die before the other, all assets shall pass to my remaining daughter or on to my sister, Nina."

I took a deep breath.

"What assets are listed?" Gran asked.

"I hereby leave my daughters all my properties along with their keys, all assets bestowed upon my father Duncan McGregor. Including a collection of weapons and the key to the archives." I rambled off a list of different things. Then noticed a note at the bottom that read: *Cassie, I've enclosed this letter. Do not read this to anyone. It's meant for only you.*

"Is that it?" Gran wanted to know.

"There's another message. Cal Thorne. You are the father of my daughter, Cassie. But I leave you only disappointment. My desire is for Cassie to become the slayer she is meant to. I don't want you to train her. She has no need for a magus. No slayer does. You'd only hold her back like you did with me." I looked up and Cal's expression darkened.

He seemed just as surprised at Estelle's "fuck you" from beyond the grave.

"It seems we must abide by my daughter's wishes." Gran gave the elves a smug look. "Cassie, get on with the next statement."

My hands shook as I opened my sister's statement. "I, Olivia…Grace Morgan." Just seeing her name made my chest ache. "… Leave my assets to my sister, Cassie. Including all royalties, copyrights to my music and their use. I ask that my next album is released. Cass, you always inspired me to be better. And I want to share my music with the world. No matter what you hear, please don't think badly of me, little sis. I, Olivia Grace Morgan, and Estelle Morgan McGregor proclaim all of our assets still belong to Cassie Morgan."

Tears stung my eyes.

"Well, neither statement can be disputed," Silvy spoke up. "I'd say we're done here."

"Estelle was —"

"Olivia Morgan is still a murderer," the council leader spoke up.

"Their assets belong to my family," Gran snapped.

"You know what." I stood up. "You can argue about the technicalities of my mother and sister's legacy statements all you want. But they made their wishes clear. As far as I'm concerned, we're done here." I grabbed the paperwork and left before anyone could say another word.

My mind raced as I made my way out of the castle. I wished I had brought my transpo bracelet with me. At least then I would have been able to transport myself back to the North Tower.

"Cassie, wait!" Ash called after me.

I groaned. I'd hoped he wouldn't follow me. As much as I knew we needed to talk, now wasn't the time I wanted to do it. I didn't know how to feel about that kiss. My emotions felt too all over the place to know what the hell I was feeling. I still couldn't believe my sister and birthmother had left me everything they owned.

Why did people seem so desperate to get their hands on Estelle and Liv's assets?

I reluctantly stopped and turned around to face him.

"Are you alright?" he asked.

"What do you think?" I snapped.

"Look, I'm sorry about earlier. I never should have —"

"Well, you did kiss me, and you can't take it back now."

"It never should have happened. It won't happen again, I promise."

I scoffed. "You have to admit, there's something between us, Ash. We can't keep ignoring it. You might want to pretend it's not there, but it is."

"Cass, you know the rules are there for a reason."

"Maybe you should've thought of that before you kissed me. You can't take it back." I couldn't believe him. Did I really mean so little to him? I thought we were friends, partners. Hell, we could be more than that. I couldn't deny the thought had crossed my mind more than once.

Ash looked away. "You're right, I can't. But nothing can ever happen between us. You need to know that."

"So go then. Pretend like nothing happened."

He sighed. "Cassie, don't be like that."

"Go and pretend, Ash. When you decide to stop pretending, let me know." I stormed away from him.

Tears stung my eyes, but I wouldn't let them fall. Not until I got somewhere private. I didn't know if it was the pain of his rejection or from the old wounds those legacy statements had reopened for me. Maybe both.

"Cassie?" someone else called out my name.

I gritted my teeth and spun around. To my surprise, Mum followed after me.

"Are you alright?" Mum asked.

I shook my head. "You should have told me about the legacy statements. They should have been read in private, not in front of all those people."

"I know, sweetheart. But I didn't have a choice. Not given who Estelle and Liv were." She held out a set of keys to me. "These are the keys for your mum's property. Just promise me you'll be careful this term. I don't have a good feeling about you being on this island."

CHAPTER 10

CASSIE

A couple of weeks passed and Ash and I barely spoke to each other. It felt weird avoiding each other like that. But I couldn't say that I wanted to see him either. Things felt so messed up since our kiss, but Ash was the one who had to go and ruin our friendship. I only hoped we could eventually get past this.

So I texted him about coming on patrol with me tonight. He'd come on patrol a couple of times but had been making excuses not to come. I couldn't say I minded because things felt too awkward between us whenever he was around.

After a couple of minutes, he replied and told me to have a night off.

A night off. Ha! Ash had to have gone bloody mad. I didn't have time for a night off.

Tonight I had to patrol no matter what. Just because he chose to neglect his duties didn't mean I had to. Lucy didn't seem to mind coming with me on patrols and Ivy sometimes joined us as well so she could conduct more experiments.

Ash hadn't told me how the case was going or even if the case was still open. My mind went to Avery again. All of the messages I'd sent her had been left unanswered. Funny, Elora had asked me and Ash to work on Vikram's case yet Ash completely shut me out. I still wanted to find out what had happened to Vikram. But if Ash didn't want my help, so be it. I'd just do my own digging around.

Why wouldn't Avery answer? Why appear to me if she didn't want to talk? Why even come here if she wasn't enrolled at the academy or working on the island? My mind raced with questions. Nothing made any sense.

I headed back to my room in the North Tower to do some more digging. I'd already checked all of Avery's social media accounts in more depth and under possible aliases. She hadn't been active on them in several months.

Financial records were harder to get into, but I knew a few ways of getting into them without triggering any alarms. Or breaking any supernatural laws. Going through my usual checks revealed nothing. Ash didn't seem interested in investigating Avery either. He didn't believe I'd even seen her.

If I couldn't count on him, I'd just have to get help from someone else. So I headed out to the great library in the academy's castle. Murphy flew alongside me.

The librarian hadn't been happy when Murphy came with me last term, but I couldn't leave him in the forest all the time. Besides, I was working on his behavioural issues.

The great library was a massive room with high arched diamond-paned windows. The bookcases reached from floor-to-ceiling and everything was all solid wood. The place smelt like old books and furniture polish.

The librarian, a dark-haired elf woman, at the front desk glowered at me when she caught sight of Murphy but didn't say anything.

Murphy settled on my shoulder.

Be good, I told him. The last thing I needed was for him to start creating more chaos. If he made a mess of things in here, I would probably get banned from the library.

Books were stacked from floor-to-ceiling.

Heavy old tomes filled each row. I moved past the bookcases and headed to the back of the library. I spotted Lucy hauling several books off the shelf and piling them up. Then she flapped her gossamer wings and flew into the air so she could grab more.

I didn't say anything to her. Best not to disturb Lucy when she was in her element. She always got annoyed when people did that. I knew that from experience.

Moving deeper into the library, I passed by other students who all had books, tablets or laptops open.

Finally, I spotted Mike in the corner. Typical Mike. He always liked hiding away. Mike Logan had a mop of dark hair, and wore his usual chequered shirt and blue jeans. We had been friends for a few years and even dated for a few weeks a couple of years ago. He'd been my only relationship, but we learnt quickly that we worked better as friends rather than as a couple. We were too different and both wanted different things.

"Hey." I shook his shoulder. "Long time no see."

Mike jumped. "Whoa, Cassie, you scared me. I wondered if I would run into you again." He grinned at me. "Wow, it's been ages. How've you been?"

"Sorry, I was hoping we could talk." I avoided his question as I didn't know how to describe how I'd been. I'd lost my sister, now it felt like I'd lost Ash too. "I need your help with something."

It was nice to have one bloke who was happy to see me. Mike and I still texted each other sometimes. He'd kept in touch over the summer wanting to know if I was okay after everything that happened with Liv. I'd only replied a couple of times because I had been so busy spending time with Ash. Maybe I should have kept in contact more. Just because Mike and I didn't really work as a couple didn't mean we couldn't still be good friends.

"Sure. What do you need?"

"To find someone. I spotted her in the great hall on the first day of term, but there's no record of her coming to the island." I didn't know why I kept coming back to Avery. But her appearance on the day of Vikram's death still puzzled me. I needed answers as to why she'd been there and why I hadn't heard from her since.

"Wow, you're still doing PI stuff then?" Mike's eyes widened. "I thought you might have given up."

I frowned at him. "Why?" Me being a PI

had always been a point of contention in our relationship. That was one of the main reasons why I didn't bother with romantic relationships much. If people couldn't accept me for who and what I was, then what was the point?

He shrugged. "Dunno. Just figured you were working with the Elhanan now given how secretive you've been lately. I thought that was why I hadn't heard back from you much over the summer."

"What do you mean?" I furrowed my brow.

"Working with the Elhanan is secretive enough. And you didn't tell me much of what you did over the summer."

He had a point. I hadn't told Mike much of what I'd been doing. He didn't know I was a slayer either. I'd never talked much about my birth mother or my heritage when we were together.

"I'm-I'm sorry. I just couldn't talk then. Things have been rough since…you know." Murphy pressed his head against my cheek and purred.

"I'm here — if you want to talk. I'm sorry about what happened to your sister. Even if you're with Ash, I'm still your friend."

"Wait, what? I'm not with Ash. We're just

friends." Hell, I couldn't even be sure we were that any more given how much he'd been avoiding me. That hurt more than anything. That he could just throw our friendship away over one kiss.

"Really?"

"Yeah."

"But weren't you living together? I thought things must be pretty serious between the two of you. You always said you'd never tie yourself to anyone."

I flinched at that. "That's...complicated. Look, sorry I haven't been much of a friend lately. Rest assured, there's nothing between me and Ash. We were just roommates and working together." Then I wondered why it mattered to him so much. I knew Mike had always been more invested in our relationship than I'd been. I wasn't a long-term relationship type of person.

"You could make it up to me. How about dinner or a drink tonight? I could help you with your case." Mike grinned. "It will be just like old times."

I hesitated. I couldn't miss patrolling tonight. "We could hang out now if you're not busy. I've got time before my next class."

"Okay, who do you need help finding?" Mike turned his attention back to his computer and braced his hands over the keyboard.

"Avery Devlin." If anyone could help me track down my old friend, it would be him. All of my usual searches had drawn a blank so I knew I needed some outside help.

"What'd she do?"

Again, I hesitated. How much should I tell him? I didn't want to go into details about Ash's case. That stuff was private. It wasn't that I didn't trust Mike. But he had never been very supportive of me becoming a private investigator.

"I saw Avery recently and since then I can't contact her. Finding her is super important."

"Is she missing?"

"Maybe."

"So is this a case or not?"

"It's complicated." I still felt hesitant about sharing too much with him. Besides, I didn't know if Avery was missing, dead or whatever.

"I thought you trusted me?"

"I do. Look, she's…a possible suspect in a crime. Or a possible victim. I need to find her, okay?" I couldn't really tell him any more than that. But I knew he would want more answers. I wouldn't divulge details about Ash's case, though.

Mike tapped away on his keyboard. "What

kind of records? Social media?"

"Done that and it was a dead end. Can you check student and academy records? I wanna make sure they haven't been tampered with." I'd tried searching through them myself but hadn't found anything. Neither had Ash.

"Cass, the Elhanan's security is —"

"Nothing you haven't faced before, right?" I flashed him a smile.

Mike shook his head. "Cassie, I need my place here at the academy. I can't risk my scholarship just to help you."

"You know I wouldn't ask if it weren't important. Please. I've got no one else to help me with this."

"Not even Ash?"

I scowled at the mention of Ash. "No, he won't help me. He's too absorbed in his latest case."

"Okay, I'll see what I can find." Mike tapped away on his keyboard then turned his screen to face me. "There's no Avery Devlin in any recent records for people who have come or gone from the island."

"What about a week or two prior?"

Mike pressed a few keys. "Nothing."

"What about someone with a similar name?"

"Would she use a different name?"

I shrugged. "Maybe, but she didn't even tell me she was coming here. Which is weird." I bit my lip and thought back to some possible aliases she might use. "Try the names Mercy Devlin and Avery Evans."

Mike tapped away on his keyboard again and shook his head. "Still nothing. How do you know her?"

"Mum investigated when her family was killed a few years ago." I leaned forward to peer at the screen and Murphy growled as I got closer to Mike.

Mike leapt to his feet, almost tipping his chair over. "Geez, do you have to bring him here?"

Murphy had never liked Mike. Odd, he never acted that way around other guys. Especially not Ash. Murphy loved him.

"Yeah, he's my dragon. I can't just leave him. Besides, you're still a stranger to him. Why don't you pet him and say hi? Try to relax. He won't hurt you."

Mike glanced at my dragon. "But he is —" He straightened but didn't reach out to touch Murphy. "Hi, Murphy."

Murphy, say hi to Mike.

Murphy growled and the spikes on his back went up. As they always did when he warned of potential threats. Goddess, what was wrong with him? It was just Mike. He'd never been a threat to me.

"Murphy, go see Lucy." I moved him onto the table. Murphy's eyes flared with light as he snarled at Mike again. "Murphy, go. Now!" I pointed in the opposite direction. Maybe it'd be better if he went away for a while. I wasn't ready to leave Mike yet and having Murphy around would just make things more awkward.

His head drooped; his spikes went down and he whined. Almost as if I'd scolded a child.

Go! I crossed my arms. *You can't growl at people for no good reason. He's a friend. If you want someone to be angry at, go and growl at Ash. Maybe that would get him to speak to us again.*

Murphy didn't budge.

"I'm sorry. He's in an awkward dragon adolescent phase." I picked Murphy up and carried him away until he flew out of my arms. "Go now." Murphy flapped his wings and perched on a shelf just out of my reach.

I gave up. *Fine, stay up there if you want to. Just don't bother anyone with your presence.*

"He doesn't like me." Mike sighed.

"He doesn't know you. Trust me, he'll come round." I glowered up at Murphy.

Mike sat back down. "Definitely no trace of

her records at the academy."

"What about CCTV? There must be footage of people coming on and off the island."

Ash had already looked at CCTV around the scene where we had found the body but refused to show me footage of the rest of the island. He thought it was a waste of time, despite my insistence.

"I can, but it could take hours to go through."

"Come on, I know you have a program that could do it in minutes." I gave him my best pleading look.

Mike chuckled. "Maybe you haven't changed as much as I thought."

"Thanks." I ruffled his hair.

"You know, I've kind of missed this. We should hang out more often."

"Yeah, we should." It felt good to have someone on my side for a change and someone who actually wanted to help me. Lucy and Ivy did what they could but they didn't have the technical skills that Mike had.

I stayed with Mike whilst he kept scanning through data. We chatted and I almost forgot about Murphy. A few hours later, we still hadn't found any sign of Avery.

"What about footage of the great hall on

the first day of term?" Ash had only given me a quick look at that.

"Cass, as fun as this has been I have work to do."

"I just need you to find me the footage. Avery was a few rows in front of me."

Mike sighed. "I need to learn to say no to you."

"Come on, that would be boring." I grinned at him. "Plus, you always enjoyed saying yes to me from what I remember."

Mike brought up the footage of the hall and zoomed into where I sat with Lucy and Ivy. "What does your friend look like?"

I groaned. "I don't see her. She's heavily tattooed and had purple and turquoise hair. So she should be pretty easy to spot."

"Me either. Are you sure —"

"Yeah, I know I saw her." Damn, I hope he didn't doubt me as well. I didn't just imagine seeing Avery in the hall. I had waved at her. Heck, I'd spoken to her in the alleyway. How could she does disappear into thin air? It still made no sense. With my slayer abilities, I should have been able to see through a glamour or spell if someone had been disguised as her. I still couldn't fathom why she wouldn't come out of hiding and talk to me again. Nor could I imagine how she'd be involved in Vikram's death either.

"You said your powers have been kind of weird."

"Mike…" I stopped when I spotted myself waving. "There! Zoom in so I can see who is a few rows in front of me."

He did as I asked. Nothing. Avery didn't appear anywhere on the footage.

"That's not possible." I shook my head. It looked like I'd been waving at an empty space. But that made no sense. How could I have imagined her?

"She's not there, Cass. I've checked the footage from every angle."

I slumped back onto my seat. "Who the hell did I see then?"

"I don't know. Come on, let's go and grab some dinner." Mike squeezed my hand. "We could both do with a break. Besides, I have a more powerful computer in my room. I can do some more digging into the footage and see what I can come up with. For what it's worth I do believe you saw someone. Maybe she was there as an astral projection or something."

I guessed that was possible. Avery was a spirit witch. She could have travelled there in spirit to come and see me and shielded herself from everyone else.

We headed out and Murphy flew alongside us. He kept a watchful eye on Mike. We headed to the food court and chatted more. I plied Murphy with plenty of steak which settled him.

"I can't remember the last time we had fun like this," Mike remarked.

"My frustrating case is fun?" I scoffed.

"No, I meant us hanging out like this. I've missed you, Cass." He caressed my cheek.

I so didn't have time for romance. "Mike…" Murphy began growling again and a chill ran over my senses.

What the hell? Was someone following us?

A shadow shot past me and something knocked me to the ground.

"Oh, goddess, Cassie, there's a body." Mike gasped.

CHAPTER 11

ASH

Getting a call about another body was the last thing I wanted. How could someone else be dead? And why? My mind raced. This showed Vikram's death couldn't have just been an accident. Too bad I still couldn't prove that.

Worse still, Cassie just had to be the one to find the body again. No way could I keep her name out of it this time. She tried calling me first. I'd been ignoring her calls, so she had called Tye instead, who contacted me. Tye gave me a lecture about not answering phone calls and I knew I couldn't avoid her forever, but it felt easier this way. Sooner or later I would have to talk to her. Guess it would have to be now.

I found her outside the food court with a

pale looking Mike Logan.

What were they doing together?

I didn't know why it bothered me so much. But I found it odd since she hardly spoke to Mike anymore. Or at least I didn't think she did.

As I drew closer, I caught Mike's scent on her body and something inside me growled. My inner demon had woken up and it wasn't happy. Curse it, my demon side had been becoming stronger recently. It was one of the reasons why I'd stayed away from Cassie because I feared it might turn on her. I'd been bitten by a demon as a child and its essence had become part of me. Meaning I changed once a month and could take on another form if I chose to. I always wore a spelled bracelet to repress the demon. Cassie was one of the only people who even knew about my demon side.

Why did being around her seem to set it off? Usually her presence settled the demon down.

"You need to be more careful," I muttered as I went over to her.

"I don't go around looking for dead bodies, Ash." Cassie scoffed and glared at me. "I'm amazed you actually showed up."

I ignored that jibe and motioned for her to

move away from Mike so we could talk in private. To my surprise, she complied. I didn't need Mike overhearing details about the case. "This guy is one of Vikram's friends. Spoke to him again the other day." I blew out a breath. "Was he in the food court with you?"

She shook her head. "No. Before you ask, no, I haven't talked to him or any of Smi-Vikram's friends today."

"Good. You're a witness. Did you see Avery again?"

"No, I haven't seen her since I found Smi-Vikram."

"You both need to make statements at the tower. And, Cass, you need to stop working on this case."

"What?" She gaped at me.

"You're a witness. You know you can't help out on an investigation now."

"No, I'm part of this. You can't shut me out!" she snapped. "Oh wait, you've been doing nothing but that recently. How are you supposed to be my magus if you keep avoiding me?"

"Just focus on other stuff. Okay?"

Cal's warning ran through my mind about not getting romantically involved with Cassie. I couldn't deny my feelings for her had grown over the summer. But I couldn't afford to let those feelings get in the way of our jobs.

Maybe I should step back from being her magus. No, I couldn't. Besides, it was normal for slayers and Magi to get close. But no way would we make the same mistake her parents had. Things would be awkward for a while, but I hoped we would find a way back to where we'd had been before I messed up and kissed her.

"Oh, you mean the stuff you don't have time for now? Are you gonna quit being my magus too? Actually, maybe that's a good idea. Maybe I should just tell Cal how you haven't been patrolling once since —"

"Of course not. But maybe some time apart would do us both good."

Cassie shook her head. "Why? You're supposed to be my partner."

"I am, but —"

"But what? You said we can't be together. Fine. Whatever." She gritted her teeth and looked away. "I'm fine with that. Why can't we go back to normal now? Why do you keep avoiding me?"

"Because... Nothing." I turned away from her but she caught hold of my arm.

"You need to get over yourself, Ash. Either make a decision and be my magus again, or I'm telling Cal. Your choice. I'm done with this shit," Cassie snapped. "Maybe Estelle was right. Maybe I'm better off not having any magus. All you do is hold me back."

I flinched at her words and went over to Mike. I couldn't get into this with her. Not right now. "Can you tell me what you saw?"

Cassie and Murphy stormed off.

"We-we found the body," Mike stuttered.

"Yeah, but did you see anyone around? Or did you see the victim beforehand?"

"No, Cassie and I came out of the food court. We were talking. I almost kissed her then…" Mike shuddered. "I've never seen a dead body before."

My jaw tightened. Great. No wonder I could smell him on her.

"How long were you and Cassie in the food court?"

Mike shrugged. "An hour or so. I was helping her with a case."

"Well, don't. Whatever she's working on can't interfere with an investigation." I waved him away.

"I don't know what's going on between you and Cassie. But you're an idiot," Mike remarked before walking off.

Tye arrived and took the body away after I was done looking around the scene.

The latest victim was Mark Budman. An elf

with a big ego and low-level magic from what I could tell.

I spent the next hour interviewing potential witnesses. Everyone had been in the food court around the time of the death. No leads. Why didn't anyone see anything? Both victims had been killed in daylight at busy times of the day. Someone had to have seen something. Anyone could have wanted him dead, though.

First, I had to get the cause of death. I found nothing so far to prove that Vikram had been murdered. Maybe it was time for some more outside help.

I headed off to find Ivy. It'd be a while before Tye got any kind of test results back. Maybe I did need to start using outside resources. Cal wouldn't be happy if he found out and I didn't want to blow this case. Still couldn't believe I was doing this.

I headed into the lab and found Ivy staring into a microscope. The lab was all state-of-the-art equipment, pristine white surfaces and stainless steel.

"Hey, Ivy."

She jumped. "What is it with visitors today?" She groaned. "I'm working here, elf boy."

"Ivy, will you come to the tower and run

some tests with Tye?"

Ivy stared at me as if I'd gone mad. "Are you serious?"

"I could sneak you in." I knew that sounded ridiculous, but I couldn't afford to have this case ruled as an accidental death, not if it turned out to be a potential murder.

Ivy snorted. "Yeah right. You must have gone insane."

"Come on, I'm desperate. I can't get any more evidence on Vikram's case. If we don't find anything on this, it will be ruled as an accident as well. I wondered if you could run some tests for me but keep things quiet."

"No way can I sneak into the enforcers' tower. Believe me, I've tried already. Several times."

"You helped on tests before and if anyone can help me, I know it's you." I gave her my best pleading look.

She rolled her eyes. "Great, you sound just like Cassie. I can't keep running secret tests for you on the sly. I've got a scholarship to think of."

"Wait, Cassie asked you to perform tests?"

Ivy flinched. "I never said that."

"Of course she did." I sighed. "What's she got you testing? Have you still been doing tests from the samples you got from Vikram?"

"No." She looked away, but I could tell she was lying.

"Ivy, you owe me and Cassie. We made sure you didn't get into trouble last term."

"Cassie said I shouldn't work with you anymore. Said you were being a complete arsehole. I don't know what's going on between the two of you, but you need to sort it out." Ivy frowned at me. "Did you two have an argument or something?"

"Or something. It's complicated between us. Don't worry about it." I shook my head. "Just tell me what you've been working on."

Her shoulders slumped. "Just tests to identify different magics. Looks like your first victim got hit with a mix of shadow magic and wild magic. Fascinating combo. Not sure how someone could have managed that."

"How do you know that?" I furrowed my brow.

Being killed by wild magic wasn't that uncommon if a lot of it leaked out or if someone tried to cross into the Nether Realm. But shadow magic was only used by dark elves. Or Drow as they were more commonly known.

"I have tested pretty much all kinds of magic. It's not as hard as you think," Ivy explained. "Except the Elhanan are sticklers sticking to the rules and never think outside the box."

"I brought a sample from the second victim. Can you run it for me?"

"Does the Elhanan know you're doing this?"

"Not exactly." I couldn't risk telling them anything as I knew they wouldn't approve of these tests.

Ivy grinned. "Cassie is rubbing off on you."

"Look, I just want to find the killer before anyone else gets hurt."

"There's a second victim?" Ivy gasped. "Wow, when did that happen? I thought Vikram was the only victim?"

"Yeah. Surprised Cassie didn't tell you."

"She called me earlier. Sounded pissed off. What did you do to upset her?"

"Nothing."

"You must've done something. But all couples argue. You should hurry up and work it out. It's not natural for you two be arguing."

"We're not a couple."

"Yeah, right." Ivy rolled her eyes. "I'll get to work on these tests. You'd better go if you don't want anyone seeing you here."

After more interviews and paperwork, I left the tower later that night and headed off to find Cassie at the North Tower. "Hey, Cassie around?" I asked Lucy as I walked in.

I decided we needed to talk and try and clear the air with each other. I had no idea what I was going to say. And things hadn't gone well when we talked earlier so I knew she wouldn't be happy to see me.

"She's up in her room, but I think she's about to go out." Lucy inclined her head towards the spiral staircase.

"Slaying? I thought she was having a night off?" I'd half hoped she would have a night off. I didn't like the idea of her being out there alone, even if she did have Lucy and possibly Ivy with her. Maybe she was right. I would have to make a choice about whether to continue being her magus or not.

Lucy shook her head. "Don't think she's going slaying."

"Luce, are you sure you can watch Murphy tonight?" Cassie called down the stairs. "You know he doesn't like Mike."

"Don't worry, Murphy won't spoil your big date," Lucy called back.

Big date? What date? Cassie didn't date. Not in all the months we'd gotten to know each other again.

"Oh, didn't you know?" Lucy asked. "Goddess, I'm sorry, Ash."

"Why? You don't need to be."

Lucy narrowed her eyes at me. "What's going on between the two of you? I know it's more than just a falling out. Something happened, didn't it?"

Cassie came in wearing a short black dress and heels. "Ash, what are you doing here?"

"Er... We've got some slayer stuff to take care of."

"You just told me to take a night off!" She crossed her arms.

"Yeah, but...things have changed. We need to do research. The killer could be something from the Nether Realm." I rubbed the back of my neck. "With the second death, we can't just ignore this."

"You said you didn't want me involved in the case."

"No, I said I didn't want you working on the case alone. I didn't say you can't work with me on the down low. If the killer came from the Nether Realm, we need to work together. Which means I still need to be your magus."

"And you have proof of that?" Cassie arched a brow.

"No, it's more like a hunch but —"

"Good, have fun researching then." Cassie pulled on her jacket. "I'm going for a drink.

And I'm not just going to come running every time you decide you actually need me. Make your damn mind up, Ash."

"Hey, wait a minute. You know how important slayer stuff is."

"You told me to take a break so I am. Bye." She stormed off and headed out.

"Did you to have an argument?" Lucy wanted to know. "She's been pissed off for the past few days."

I ran a hand through my hair. "I told her she can't work on the case. And maybe we should have a break from each other. But obviously that can't happen. If this killer or whatever it came from the Nether, we need to work together. We need to put our feelings aside and solve this case."

"Why do you need a break from each other? You spent the entire summer together."

"Yeah, but... Never mind. Guess I'll do research on my own."

"I could help, if you want. Goddess knows I don't have anyone to go on dates with at the moment since my girlfriend is away for the next few weeks."

"You're not allowed."

"Who says? Some stupid slayer rules laid out a thousand years ago?" Lucy scoffed.

"Too bad, I'm helping."

I waved my hand. A huge pile of old tomes appeared on the kitchen table. "Let's get started."

"What are all these?" Lucy's eyes went wide.

"Grimoires and old records. Accounts from Magi who recorded what their slayers fought against."

"Wow, you have a lot of records."

"Let's get started then."

A few hours went by and my eyes blurred. Cassie still hadn't come back either. I glanced at my watch. Three a.m.

"Are you waiting for her to come back?" Lucy yawned.

"No. Well, maybe. I didn't think she would be gone so long. We should call it a night."

"Her being with Mike bothers you."

"I never said that."

"You don't have to. I see the way you look at her."

"You know we're not allowed to be romantically involved."

"That doesn't change the way you feel, Ash. If you care about her —"

"No! I mean, I don't. Not in the way you think. Thanks for your help." I got up, but Lucy grabbed my arm.

"Hey, are you are going to tell me what happened between the two of you?"

"I thought Cassie would have told you."

Lucy's eyes gleamed. "I knew something happened! And no, she wouldn't tell me anything. No matter how hard I tried to get it out of her. So spill. What's going on between the two of you?"

"Nothing. Nothing I want to talk about."

"Come on, Ash. You will never resolve things with each other unless you admit how you feel. I know you have feelings for her, it's written all over your face. So why can't you just tell her?"

I sighed. "Because it can never work between us. Not just because of the rules. I acted on my feelings, now look at the mess we're in. We can barely stand to be around each other."

"Feelings don't just go away. Sooner or later, one of you is going to have to admit how you feel."

CHAPTER 12

CASSIE

I couldn't believe how Ash had the audacity to come over and try to talk to me and pretend like nothing had happened. Not after how he'd been avoiding me so much lately.

Unbelievable.

I still didn't understand why he'd spouted all that nonsense about us needing a break from each other. We had to talk about that kiss sooner or later. I wasn't afraid of my feelings, but if he didn't want me, I wasn't about to wait around for him forever. Maybe it was time to move on or at least spend time with an old friend.

Going out for a drink had been Mike's idea. I wasn't sure I wanted to rekindle our old romance. We had been together a few weeks, and I hadn't been with anyone else since then.

Romance never ranked high on my list of priorities. I wasn't one of those women who needed a man to be complete.

Why had I agreed to this? I couldn't be sure. Maybe because it felt good to have someone believe me.

Ash should be the one who believed me. He was my partner. Mike was just a friend.

Mike always complained I made work a priority over him. I cared about him, but love? I couldn't be sure. I only agreed to tonight so I could have someone to talk to about the case with.

Mike wasn't an investigator, but he knew why I worked cases. And acted more supportive than Ash and the Elhanan's stupid rules.

I headed to the Magic Users Housing Block and cut down a side alley to get there quicker. I wanted to work on the case but maybe I needed a break. If I worked myself too hard, I'd be useless to everyone. Maybe Mike would be able to give me some insight on where to search for Avery next.

We headed to the island's nightclub, Nocturnal, which was owned by my aunt Delia, who everyone called Dee.

The club had a black and red retro theme and the club vibrated with energy — both magical and musical.

"Hey, stranger," someone called out and a gorgeous elf woman with long dark hair came over and hugged me.

"Hi, Auntie. It's been a while."

"A while? It's been ages. I haven't seen you since the summer holidays. You live on this island for a good part of the year, yet you don't come and visit enough." Dee pouted.

"I'm sorry, you know I get busy with cases and stuff." I gave her a smile. "It's great to see you. How have things been here at the club?"

"Busy as usual. Who's your friend? Surprised you aren't with that sexy elf of yours. You're usually attached at the hip." Dee smiled.

Mike waved from the bar where he stood waiting to order us drinks.

"That's Mike, he's a friend. And Ash isn't my elf." I scowled at the mention of him. Jeez, why did she have to mention Ash? He was the one thing I wanted to forget about tonight.

Dee laughed. "Yeah, right. I've never seen you with anyone the way you are with him." She glanced over at Mike. "Didn't he used to be your boyfriend?"

I almost groaned. Great, trust her to remember that. "Yeah, but I don't have time for romantic relationships."

"Come on, Cass. Just because you're the slayer doesn't mean you have to be celibate. You're young. You deserve to have fun."

"I'm trying. I'll…"

Dee grabbed my arm and dragged me over to the bar. "What are you two having? Drinks are on the house."

"I'll just have a Pepsi. Mike?"

"I'll have a beer."

"How's it been being back at the academy?" Dee asked. "You still working with the enforcers?"

"It's been…busy. Listen, Auntie Dee, have you seen this person around?" I pulled out my phone and showed her a picture of Avery. It was a couple of years old and her hair was long and black in it, but it still looked like her.

Auntie Dee frowned. "Yeah, she was a student here last year, I think. I always remember faces. Think I saw her with Liv once."

"Wait, when last year? When I was here at the academy?"

Dee shrugged. "No, before that, I think."

"Please try to remember. Do you remember what she was doing with Liv? It's important."

I couldn't believe I finally had a lead. None

of my searches so far had yielded any results about Avery. If only I'd come here sooner. This proved Avery had been on the island at some point. But why couldn't I find any records of her? People weren't allowed to live or come on to the island without good reason.

Dee shook her head and someone brought over our drinks. "Sorry, I can't remember. I think she and Liv were just hanging out together. Why? Is this part of another case? Goddess, you're so much like Nina. It's disturbing. You know you don't always have to work or worry about slay —"

"Thanks, Auntie Dee. See you later."

Mike and I spent most of the night just sitting and talking after we left the club. It felt good to catch up. Almost like it had been when we were together. Realising how tired I was, I left just as the sun came up and ducked into the alleyway.

My senses prickled in warning.

Now what? Was it too much to get a day off after weeks of constant vigilance?

Geez, Ash had been the one who'd insisted I take a break.

A tall male with pointed ears advanced towards me and growled. His blue skin shimmered under the streetlights. Great. A

Drow.

So much for a night off. I didn't have my sword with me but I did have a knife strapped to my thigh. Ash gave me the blade for my twentieth birthday.

I blew out a breath. "Here's an idea. How about you bugger off and I won't have to slay you?" I couldn't just let a Drow keep wandering around the island and wouldn't, but he didn't need to know that.

The Drow growled and lunged towards me.
Great. Just great.

I dodged him when he made a grab for me. I punched him in the face and sent him staggering. Fumbling underneath my dress, I searched for my knife.

The Drow backhanded me so hard I slammed into the wall.

Why did Drow have to be stronger than normal elves? You'd think having no souls would make them weaker.

I grunted and staggered to my feet. My head spun with a nauseating wave of dizziness.

What the hell was wrong with me? The dizziness grew worse and everything around me spun. What the hell?

The Drow grabbed me by the throat and lifted me off my feet.

"Cassie?" someone behind me gasped.

A quick glance revealed it to be my cousin, Jolie. I'd forgotten she lived in this block too.

I flayed about but my punches didn't make contact with anything solid.

Where the hell had my strength gone?

My eyes blurred as the Drow choked me harder.

Murphy! I yelled for him in my mind.

A streak of light shot towards us and something knocked the Drow and me to the ground. It was enough to get the Drow to let go. I coughed and gasped for breath.

Murphy and the Drow thrashed against each other.

It took me a second to realise Murphy had grown in size and tore into the Drow with his teeth.

"Jolie, my…knife…" I croaked.

My cousin stood there frozen. Murphy and the Drow grappled for control.

I crawled along the ground but couldn't spot my knife anywhere.

Damn it! I raised my hand to use my magic.

Nothing happened.

What the hell?

Now I knew there had to be something wrong with me.

"Jolie!" My voice came out stronger.

That brought her to her senses and she rushed over to me. "Are you hurt?"

The Drow shoved Murphy away.

I glanced around for a potential weapon. Found none. "Jo, use your power."

"What?"

"Now! Get us out of here!"

Jolie gripped my arm and transported us out. Light blazed around us and the heavy mist of the other side surrounded us.

I gasped and took a deep breath. "Jo, there's something wrong with my powers."

"What? How…?"

"Never mind. Take us back. I can't leave Murphy with that Drow."

I still had to kill the Drow. No way could I let it wander around the island hurting people.

"You can't fight without your powers."

"Guess you'll have to help. Now let's go." I gasped again as we reappeared in the alleyway.

Murphy flung himself at me. "Good boy." I patted him then pushed him away. The Drow had vanished. "Damn it, Murph, can you find my…" Murphy had something between his teeth. My knife. "Good boy. Now I need to find the Drow."

Light blurred as Murphy dragged me out of the alleyway.

I yelped. "Murphy!" My head spun and my

stomach recoiled. Bile rose in my throat and I thought I'd be sick.

He ignored me and instead we reappeared close to the food court.

Great. A Drow out in the open. Why hadn't it broken into the housing block?

"Murph, bring me the Drow."

He darted off and the Drow soon appeared staggering out. I ducked into an alleyway as Murphy dragged the Drow towards me.

The Drow grappled with my dragon.

"Murph, pin him down!"

Murphy flapped his wings and knocked the Drow to the ground. I shoved my knife through the Drow's chest and his body disintegrated.

Ash had mentioned the knife had the power to destroy its intended target.

I breathed a sigh of relief. "Thanks, boy. Come on, let's get out of here."

I stumbled into the North Tower.

"Murphy, finally! I panicked when you disappeared." Lucy paled when she saw me. "Are you okay?"

"No, my powers are gone." I slumped onto the sofa. Murphy wrapped himself round my shoulders.

"What? How?"

"I don't know. I fought a Drow and it nearly killed me."

"Slayers can't lose their powers, can they?" Lucy handed me some healing balm. "Here. You've got some nasty bruises around your neck."

"I've never heard of a slayer losing their powers." I took the balm and rubbed some around my aching throat. Normally I healed fast, but if my powers were gone I might not.

"Did the Drow do something to you?"

I shook my head. "Other than choking me, no."

"Did it use magic?"

"When elves become Drow, they lose their powers. They just keep their strength and speed."

"Wow, I didn't know that." Lucy's eyebrows rose. "Did you call Ash?"

I snorted. "We not talking. Besides, he's busy, remember?

"What about Mike? What were you doing with him for most of the night?"

"Mike would never hurt me. We just stayed in his room after we went for a drink at the island's nightclub."

"Hello, club. Perfect place for women to get drugged."

I shook my head. "Human women maybe.

I only had one drink at the club and my aunt is pretty vigilant about checking all the drinks. Besides, Mike'd never do anything to hurt me."

"Still we should take a blood sample. Ivy can run it and see what shows up. Are you calling Ash?"

"No. We'll have to figure this out on our own."

CHAPTER 13

CASSIE

The next morning I woke up to find my powers still pretty non-existent. This was a nightmare I wanted to wake up from. No slayer lost their powers.

What was wrong with me? I thought about calling Ash, but I didn't want to face him again. Besides, he hadn't acted like a magus lately. What good would he be now?

"Something's wrong with me. My powers are still gone," I told Ivy and Lucy when I went down to the kitchen.

Lucy gaped at me from where she sat eating a bowl of cornflakes at the table. "Still? I thought they'd be back by now."

I slumped into the chair opposite her. "This is a nightmare!"

Ivy grabbed some bread from the toaster. "Have you called Ash?"

"No. I can't deal with Ash right now. Plus, he's the one who says we need a break from each other." I scowled. "He wouldn't help anyway. He's too wrapped up in his cases."

"But his job is also to help you," Ivy pointed out.

"Not anymore. Maybe Estelle's right. Maybe I'm better off without magus. I need to see if I can manage without one."

"Tell us what happened."

So I sat and told them all about what happened. How I had gone to meet Mike and had been attacked by the Drow.

"Did the Drow scratch you or something?" Ivy asked.

"No, and even if they did, no slayer has lost their powers before." I shook my head. "I need to figure this out fast."

"Slayer records would be good," Ivy mused. "Guess you need a magus for that. Maybe try your dad rather than Ash."

That idea seemed just as bad as seeing Ash. If not worse.

"No way. Then I'd have to tell him Ash isn't my acting magus anymore. That's more trouble than it's worth." I turned to Ivy. "Did your tests show anything?"

Ivy shook her head. "Nope. You didn't show any sign of drugs or harmful substances."

"Ivy could run some more tests, but I think we need some slayer knowledge," Lucy said. "I'll talk to Ash if you want me to."

I groaned. "I can't deal with him right now." I blew out a breath. "There might be another way. I have access to slayer knowledge."

"What? How?" Lucy wanted to know.

"My birth mum left me her keys to her house in Elfhame. It includes archives and a huge library."

"Sounds awesome." Lucy grinned. "Haven't you been there since you got the keys?"

"I'm not sure I want to go back there. It's where Estelle…" I said. "Guess I don't have a choice now."

"Good thing you and I have a study day. Let's go."

"Wait, I want to come too," Ivy spoke up.

"Don't you have work and classes?" I frowned at her.

"Nothing that can't wait. Plus, it's not every day you get to visit a dead slayer's home."

The three of us headed out to the transport stone along with Murphy.

I felt sick to my stomach at the thought of going back to my childhood home. I hadn't been there since the night Estelle was killed. Never really gave it much thought either. Mum collected my things for me when I went to live with her. Liv had mentioned going back a couple of times. Said she'd wanted to find out what happened to Estelle. She never told me if she'd found anything there.

From what I remembered Estelle's death had been ruled as "being killed in action". I'd never questioned it, not the way Liv had. I just never realised how deep her desire to find the truth had been until she died too.

In truth, I never wanted to step foot in Estelle's house again. It brought back memories of the night she died. I didn't remember much about that nor did I want to remember it. But now I didn't have a choice. I had to get my powers back or I'd be useless the next time a Drow attacked.

"Sure you want to do this?" Lucy asked as we approached the stone.

"Nope, but let's get it over with." I grabbed her hand as she grabbed Ivy's. I used my free hand to touch the stone.

Light blazed around us and a buzzing sound echoed through my ears.

I gasped as we all stepped onto a patch of dead grass.

"Wow, that always feels weird." Lucy clutched her stomach and Ivy looked a little paler than usual.

"Let's go." I motioned for them to follow and moved over the grass as I headed past the trees.

"Hey, where's the house?" Lucy ran to keep up with me.

"It's not far." It surprised me I remembered which way to go.

It'd been eight years since I'd last been here. My memories of this place were fragmented thanks to Estelle cloaking them. Maybe I could find out why now. I still couldn't fathom why she'd do that. Mum hadn't been able to give me any answers on that either.

As I moved past the trees a massive house with grey stone walls came into view.

"Wow, is that a house or a fortress?" Lucy laughed.

"A bit of both." I grimaced and pulled out my keys.

"Hey, we're right here with you." Ivy squeezed my arm. "I know how hard it is to face your past."

"We are not going in the house." I shook my head. "There's a door to the archives and library." I trudged over the gravel.

Murphy flew over and wrapped himself around my shoulders.

I shoved him away. I didn't want comforting. Instead, I needed to focus on fixing my powers and find out what had caused me to lose them. Heading over to the east tower, I felt around the bricks.

"What are you doing?" Lucy frowned.

"The doorway's concealed. Only someone with McGregor blood can open it."

"Cassie?"

A memory dragged me in. Estelle with her long purple, almost black hair stood out in front of the tower. "Today's a rite of passage. Every slayer gets to go into the archives and receive the knowledge of their ancestors."

I drew back, afraid. "What do you mean, Mama?"

"A slayer must gain all of their ancestors' knowledge. If not, then they don't deserve to be called a slayer."

"Mother, you're scaring her," another voice snapped.

"Stay out of this, Olivia."

Liv, with her lilac hair and gossamer wings stomped round the corner towards us.

"At least Cassie didn't reject her training." Estelle growled at her. "Unlike you."

"Or maybe that's because Cassie is the daughter you always wanted, right, Mama? Since she looks like an elf." Liv glared right back at her.

"Olivia, stop." Estelle grabbed Liv's arm. "This is a big day for Cassie. Don't ruin it for her."

"Right. Mustn't spoil things." Liv yanked her arm away. "Just because I never wanted to be a slayer doesn't mean…"

"Cassie." Lucy's hand on my shoulder broke me out of my memory. "Are you okay?"

"Liv knew she was a slayer," I muttered.

"What?" Lucy frowned at me.

"Liv knew she was a slayer. I knew it too. Why would I forget that?" I ran a hand through my hair.

"Your memories were cloaked. Maybe they're coming back." Lucy squeezed my arm.

"Maybe. But why wouldn't Liv tell me?"

"Perhaps she didn't want to be one," Ivy mused. "It's a tough call to put your life at risk all the time."

"She should have told me." I never realised just how much Liv had kept from me until I lost her.

I returned my attention to the tower's brickwork. Finally, something clicked and a door flashed into existence.

Turning the key, the ancient wood groaned as the door opened.

"Nice." Lucy grinned. "That's some high-level magic."

"Concealing things isn't that hard," Ivy remarked.

I ignored them as I headed up the spiral steps. To my surprise, no dust or cobwebs were to be found. No doubt Estelle had used magic to do that. She'd hated cleaning. That much I did remember.

Weird. Most of the time I'd spent here had been training and learning about my slayer heritage.

When I reached the landing, a wooden door stood closed and a shiny metallic seal sat in the middle of the door.

"What's that?" Lucy asked as she came up behind me.

"Ooh, an Andovian lock. Nice. I've never seen one before." Ivy smiled. "They're ancient. Supposed to come from the mythical realm of Andovia. The locks are spelled so only specific people can open them."

"How'd you know that?" Lucy furrowed her brow.

Ivy shrugged. "Hey, I read too; you know."

"My family have a lot of ancient artefacts." I reached out and placed my hand on the lock. After a few moments, the door swung open.

Walking inside, I took in the floor-to-ceiling rows of books, scrolls and old tablets. People would kill to get their hands on these. That was why every slayer was taught to always keep the place protected and hidden.

Lucy and Ivy screamed as they were hurtled from the doorway by a blast of light. They slumped onto the landing.

"Oh, shit. I forgot about the security in this room." I gasped as I rushed over to them.

"Jesus, Cass, you could have warned us," Ivy snapped.

"I'm sorry. I forgot people can't come in unless the magic is tuened to recognise them. Are you two okay?"

Murphy growled as he hovered by the door. He couldn't get in either.

"I'm okay, I think." Lucy groaned. "Guess your mum didn't like having guests."

"Can't you program it to let us in?" Ivy scrambled up and spun around to check if her wings were damaged.

"I don't know how to. My memories of this place and how it works are pretty are hazy."

"How are we supposed to get in then?" Lucy wanted to know.

I reached through the door and yanked Murphy inside. Murphy yelped but he didn't get blasted by anything at least.

I did the same with Lucy and Ivy and finally got them inside.

"This place is incredible," Lucy breathed. "It puts the academy's library to shame."

"Wow, what's this?" Ivy walked over to a large marble pedestal inlaid with silver buttons. "Looks like some kind of technology."

"Don't touch that," I warned. "Just be careful what you touch in here. Estelle spelled a lot of this stuff so only people with slayer blood can use them."

"Fine, what is it?"

I closed my eyes, searching for my jumbled memories.

"Focus, Cassie. This will allow you to absorb all of your ancestor's knowledge."

I opened my eyes, reached out and touched the pedestal.

"Cassie, you must be careful…" Estelle's voice ringing through my mind was the last thing I heard before everything went black.

CHAPTER 14

ASH

"You can't let them rule the second death as an accident," I flat out told Cal.

"You haven't presented any evidence to prove Vikram or this other man's death was suspicious. People do die from Nether Realm magic. It's rare, but it happens and there's nothing we can do about it." Cal leaned back in his desk chair.

"Just give me a few more days to get the test results back."

"You mean the unauthorised tests you've had Ivy Blue conducting? Yes, I know about those. I thought you knew better than that, Ash." He scowled at me. "You're playing with fire, boy. Anything you get from those tests won't be used in the case."

"I don't have a choice," I wanted to say.

"No other testing methods are yielding results," I said instead. "I need to know if they were accidents or not. I owe that to the victims."

"Ash, I don't want to see you ruin your first real case."

"I won't. I'm not. I'll have something for you in the next few days." I had to get something soon or no amount of help from Elora or Ivy would do any good.

"I'm not sure I can give you that long. We're facing a lot of pressure from the chancellor and the eleven council," Cal said. "Present something in the next twenty-four hours or the cases will be closed. We can't afford to keep wasting resources on this."

Storming off, my thoughts whirled. My reputation as an investigator wouldn't look great if both deaths were ruled Nether accidents.

Pulling out my phone, I called Ivy.

"Ash!" She answered on the first ring.

"Please tell me you've found —"

"Never mind that. Something's wrong with Cassie. You have to come and help."

"What happened?" All thoughts of the case rushed from my mind.

Something must have happened. What if Cassie was hurt and I hadn't been there to help her?

"We're at Cassie's mum's house in Elfhame. We went to the archive tower and she collapsed."

It took me a moment to realise she meant Estelle's house, not Nina's. Nina lived in Colchester in the human realm, not in the elven realm.

"Archives? Estelle's house? By the Nether, why would she go there without me? She must know how dangerous the place could be."

"Maybe because you've been an arsehole to her lately and bailed on being her magus," Lucy spoke up. "You gonna help this time or not? If you don't, we're calling Cal. You really fucked up, Ash! You should be helping, not being a total prat, feeling sorry for yourself."

"I'm on my way."

My mind raced as I transported out to the transfer stone so I could get to Elfhame.

Anything could happen to Cassie. From what she'd told me, I knew she didn't remember much about Estelle or her life before the age of twelve. I suspected Estelle cloaked her memories to protect her slayer knowledge. I didn't understand why all those memories hadn't come back yet.

Touching the transference stone, I

reappeared in Elfhame near Estelle's old house.

I hadn't been back here since I was a kid, when Estelle had been killed and I'd found Cassie unconscious. The memory haunted me for years. Especially when she left to live with her aunt. Until last year when we ran into each other again.

Damn it, why hadn't she called me? Yes, we might have been avoiding each other but I didn't think she'd go near that house again.

This was my fault. I never should have kissed her. I'd messed up our relationship and I had to fix it somehow. I didn't know how we'd find a way back from this but we had to.

I'd been an idiot to think I could ignore my magus duties. Now her life had been put at risk because of me. One way or another I would find a way to make this up to her.

Estelle's house loomed ahead of me like a silent sentinel. Its empty windows staring down like watchful eyes. The place felt cold and unwelcoming. Once it had been a happy home, now it just stood like a monument to the past. A memory to a long dead slayer.

By the Nether, I never wanted to come back here. I doubted Cassie did either. It held too many bad memories.

I refused to let the memory of Cassie lying

on the floor into my mind. That was years ago and the time had passed. It didn't mean she had been attacked. The entire house had been spelled by Estelle to keep out unwanted visitors. All of that magical security would have stayed in place even after Estelle's death. Most magic faded when someone died, but not a slayer's magic.

Heading over to the archives tower, I found the hidden door already open and visible. Cassie had to have gone up there. Running up the steps, I approached the landing and found the archive door already wide open.

"Lucy? Ivy?" I called out.

"In here, Ash," Lucy called back. "Hurry up. She still hasn't woken up."

I moved inside the room, glad none of the house's magic repelled me. Even I, as Cassie's magus, had always been restricted to which parts of the house I'd been allowed in. Estelle never allowed anyone in here apart from Cassie. From what I remembered; she didn't even allow Cal here. Not very often at least. They always argued about it when we were kids. It had always been a point of contention between the two of them.

Ivy and Lucy knelt by an unconscious Cassie on the flagstone floor.

"What happened?" I asked as I moved over to them. "Tell me everything. Don't leave anything out. This place has a lot of ancient magic in it and anything could have happened."

"She touched that pedestal and it blasted her with some kind of magic." Ivy motioned to a marble pedestal inlaid with silver buttons. "Hurry up and heal her. She's weak enough already. There's no telling what that blast might've done to her."

"Weak? What do you mean?" I furrowed my brow as I knelt down beside Cassie.

Why in the Nether would Cassie be weak? Had she already been hurt?

"She lost her powers," Lucy snapped. "Maybe if you'd been around more this would never have happened."

I winced at her words and held my hands out over Cassie. My senses roamed over her body. No slayer ever lost their powers. I would have had something like that drilled into me as a kid if they had. But none of Cal's warnings ever involved a slayer losing their powers at any point.

"Well, what's wrong with her?" Ivy demanded. "Why aren't you healing her?"

I ignored her and let my senses assess Cassie's body. To my surprise, I didn't sense any physical or internal injuries. That was something I was taught to look for when we were kids. A magus wasn't just meant to record and watch a slayer's activities. They were supposed to help them and heal them. To be there for them in times of battle. I had failed in my duty to do that.

Had the blast just knocked her unconscious?

"Come on, what's wrong with her?" Lucy asked, desperate.

Again, I ignored her. I closed my eyes and sent my senses deeper. From what I could tell, the blast hadn't injured her. So what had it done? A blast of magic shouldn't have affected a slayer that badly. She shouldn't have been unconscious more than a few seconds, if at all. Slayers were resilient. That was part of their strength and they had rapid healing powers.

"How long has she been unconscious?" I asked instead.

Lucy glanced at her watch. "Maybe ten minutes or so. What's wrong with her?" she repeated.

"Nothing, from what I can tell. She should be awake. I don't detect any sign of injury, physical or otherwise."

"What about her powers?" Lucy persisted.

"Why don't you tell me how she lost them in the first place." I gave her a hard look. "You should've called me earlier. This has never happened before."

"Would you do anything to help? As you sure as hell haven't been doing anything recently." Ivy glared at me. "You pretty much left Cassie on her own, so if anyone is to blame for this, it's you."

I gritted my teeth, but I knew I couldn't argue against that. Because it was true. "Just tell me what happened."

Lucy shrugged. "She got attacked by a Drow in the early hours of this morning. During the fight she said her powers disappeared."

I closed my eyes again and sent my senses deeper into Cassie's body. It took me a few moments to find the source of her power. Right there, in the centre of her chest. Her magic was still there, glowing like a beacon inside her. Something had to be suppressing it, but I couldn't find what.

I'd never heard of a Drow affecting a slayer like this. It had to be something else. I didn't sense any dark magic in her body.

"Have you run any tests on her?" I asked Ivy.

She nodded. "Only a blood test. I think she

expected her powers to be back by now."

"Damn it, she should have called me. I would have... Never mind." I held up my hands and sent healing energy into her body. I didn't know if it would do much good, but I knew I had to do something.

"Why is nothing happening?" Lucy frowned.

"I told you; I don't know what's wrong with her. I'm not sure my magic will do any good."

"You must be able to do something." Lucy prodded me. "Either that or call Cal. Maybe he can help."

I rose to my feet and went over to the pedestal. Placing my hand on it, I scanned it with my senses and the feel of Estelle's magic hit me hard.

"I think Cassie's mum might have done this."

"Why would she do that? Would she want to harm Cassie?" Lucy narrowed her eyes. "It seems strange to leave her an entire house just to hurt her."

"No, I don't think so. She was a tough mother, but she loved her daughters. Maybe it was to leave her a message or something."

"Weird way of leaving a message," Ivy remarked. "Why not just leave her a letter or a note? Like she did in her legacy statement?"

I winced at the reminder of Estelle's legacy statement. She told Cassie she didn't need a magus. That confused me as Estelle herself had a magus. Although she and Cal hadn't always gotten along and had a turbulent relationship. Especially after they had had a child together. Plus, I had been brought up alongside Cassie to be her magus, up until up until Estelle died.

An alarm started blaring and made us all jump. The sound jolted through me like lightning. I knew that sound well. Estelle always told us to be ready whenever that alarm sounded. My senses went on alert. Someone was here. Someone who shouldn't be here. I could feel it.

Now what? Why would anyone have come here? This place had been empty for years. Had someone somehow been alerted to Cassie coming here? If so, why? Estelle was gone.

"Stay here. I'll check it out. Get Cassie onto the sofa and try and make her comfortable. I'll be back as soon as I can." I rushed out and closed the door behind me.

"Wait, where are you going?" Lucy called after me, but I ignored her.

I'd have to take care of Cassie later. For

now, I thought she would be okay. I had left the tower's outer door open. If someone managed to get in, there was no telling what might happen.

By the Nether, why hadn't I thought to shut the door when I came in? I'd been so desperate to get to Cassie, I didn't even given it a thought.

I slipped outside and pushed the tower door shut. To my surprise, I found no one on the stairwell or outside. What triggered the alarm? What had they come here for?

CHAPTER 15

CASSIE

"Cassie, I'm sorry to hurt you like this. This is the only way I could be sure to send you a message. The only safe way to communicate with you." Estelle's voice rang through my mind. "Someone will come for you. An enemy. That's why…"

Her voice grew distant.

"Mama? Mama?" I called out.

"Remember, Cassie. All this knowledge from our ancestors is sacred," Estelle said.

I found myself back on the day I was due to receive my slayer knowledge.

"Are you willing to accept this incredible gift?" Estelle looked hopeful. "You must have an open mind and heart for this to work."

I nodded and reached out to touch the pedestal. Light blazed around me and energy jolted through my body.

"Cassie —"

Images blurred through my mind.

"Cassie..." Estelle called out to me but her voice sounded far off.

More images rushed past me.

"Cassie? Cassie, come on wake up," someone said, and a sharp pain stabbed across my face.

"I don't think hitting her is going to do any good," said another voice.

It took me a few moments to come back to myself when the images faded.

"Come on, Cass."

Something heavy climbed onto my stomach and wrapped itself around me.

"Murphy, get off me." I shoved him off and groaned.

"Thank goodness you're awake," Lucy breathed. "Are you okay?"

"What the hell happened?" Ivy wanted to know.

"I think Estelle sent me a message, but it's all jumbled." I shook my head. "She warned me someone would be coming after me."

"Who? Why?" Lucy asked.

I shrugged. "No idea. I don't think I got all of the message. I don't know why anyone would come after me either."

"Maybe they're already here." Ivy scrambled up. "An alarm went off a couple of minutes ago. Ash told us to stay with you so —"

"Wait, Ash is here?" I gaped at her. "Why would he be here?"

"You were unconscious. We had to do something," Lucy insisted.

"Right. We thought you were injured." Ivy nodded. "We couldn't wake you up."

"I'm not injured." I scowled and got up from the sofa. "You didn't need to call him." I went over to the pedestal and pressed a few buttons to bring up the house's security system.

After a few seconds, a glowing screen appeared. It showed a view of the grounds. Ash scoured around but I didn't see any sign of anyone else.

Argh, I couldn't deal with him right now.

The last thing I wanted to do was talk to him.

I scrolled through the list of people that the house in the grounds allowed access to. After a few taps, I moved Ash's energy signature to the rejection list. Light blazed over the screen and Ash vanished.

"What just happened?" Lucy came over and frowned.

"Ash isn't allowed here anymore."

"Why not?"

"Because I don't want him here. He's not my magus anymore. He made his choice."

"Cassie, I know he —"

I cut her off. "Let's just get to work on figuring out what's wrong with my powers."

A few days passed and my powers finally returned as if nothing had been wrong. Ash tried calling and texting a few times but I ignored him. I still couldn't understand why Lucy and Ivy called him just because I'd been unconscious for a while.

I didn't know what to say to him anyway. Things were still too awkward between us.

Ash believed the killer — if there was the killer — came through the Nether. I didn't see how. When things came through the Nether, they usually couldn't go back through. That's why monsters got stuck here.

I spotted Avery around a few more times but it was only brief glimpses. Last night, I saw her again. Now I had to figure out why. So I headed to Jolie's dorm and knocked on the door.

Jolie opened it and sighed. "I knew you'd show up sooner or later."

"You know about Avery?" I frowned. "Have you seen her?"

"No, but everyone in our family comes to me sooner or later. And before you ask, no I can't help you." She slammed the door in my face.

Fine, guess I'd have to ask a different relative for help. Only this one would be more complicated.

"Hi, Mum." I held up my phone so I could get a better look at her.

"Finally, I thought you were gonna call me more often?"

"I text you every day."

"Yeah, but I don't get to see you. How's school?"

"Fine, but I need your help with something." I could almost see her pointed ears perk up when I said that.

"You're working a case? When do you have time for that between classes and slayer stuff?"

"I make time for it. Don't have much choice. I need you to help me find Avery Devlin. She's missing. Auntie Dee said she was here on the island last year and briefly attended the academy for a while, but then she seemed to vanish off the face of the earth."

Mum shuffled around with papers on her desk. "Wait, Avery was living on the other side of Colchester last I heard. I don't have any missing person case files on her."

"She's not been reported missing, not officially."

"Why do need to find her?"

Great. I knew she'd ask that. I hadn't mentioned the case to her before now as I knew she wouldn't be happy.

"A couple elves have been killed on the island. And Avery was there when one of the bodies was found."

Mum swore under her breath. "Why didn't you tell me this before now? You should keep me up to date about these kinds of things. I wonder why I haven't heard anything about this from my enforcer contacts."

"I didn't want to worry you. Besides, the enforcers don't think it was murder. They just want to rule the deaths as an accident." Mum worried enough about me being at the academy as it was.

"Is Ash or Cal investigating the case?" She arched an eyebrow at me.

"Ash is. It's his first official case on his own." I scowled at the mention of his name.

"Wait, what's that look? Has something happened between you and Ash?"

I looked away. I couldn't lie to her. Especially not when she could see my face. She knew me better than anyone. Nor could I tell her that Ash and I had stopped working together. That would only lead to more unwanted questions. Questions I didn't want to answer.

"Cassie —"

"Will you help look for Avery or not?" I cut off her inevitable rant. "She hasn't been active on social media and there's no records for her for the last few months."

Mum swore again. "Of course I'll help, but you'll need to tell me what's happening. Don't give me bullshit about worrying."

"Okay."

Mum turned her attention away from the phone and tapped on her keyboard. "Maybe she's using her new identity."

"Wait, you never told me what she changed her name to."

"She's probably changed it again. I'll send you over a list of her aliases and I'll call you later if I find anything," Mum said. "What else do you know about the murders?"

I gave her a quick rundown of what little information I knew.

Mum bombarded me with more questions and told me she'd call me if she found anything. And also made me promise to call more often.

I headed out to the library that afternoon to meet Mike again. We'd been spending a lot of time together lately. Not just trying to track down Avery. It had been fun hanging out again.

I went and sat in our usual meeting spot and Murphy crash landed on the table. "I told you not to follow me." I scowled at him. "You make Mike nervous."

"Maybe it's a sign," Lucy remarked as she came over and sat beside me. She plonked a pile of books onto the table. "Maybe you shouldn't be dating Mike."

I scowled at her. "We're not dating."

"Bet he thinks you are. I don't know why you don't just talk to Ash. Try and clear the air with him."

"Don't you have studying to do?" The last thing I wanted was her pestering me about my relationship with Mike again. She seemed convinced we were dating and that couldn't be further from the truth.

"Yeah, but I can talk and study at the same time. Are we going patrolling tonight?"

Before I could answer, Ivy came strolling over to us, grinning with excitement. "I've got a new device and want to try it out. Please tell me you're going patrolling."

"Keep your voices down," I hissed at them.
"Yeah, probably. What kind of device?"

"This." Ivy pulled out a shrewd looking gun-shaped item made from various bits of metal. "It might not look like much but this thing could be revolutionary in how we fight the Drow."

I narrowed my eyes. "What does it do?"

"It should stun the Drow and keep them down long enough for me to get some samples from them. This could not only help Ash's case but it could prove useful to how you fight as well."

"I hope this works."

Lucy, Ivy and I all headed out for our routine patrol that night. It still felt strange at times not having Ash with me. I liked having my roommates around, but it didn't feel the same. Ash and I had been a team. Still this was my new way of doing things.

Plus, Lucy kept track of everything in her magus reports. I still didn't know how I would explain those to Cal yet. He would notice sooner or later that Ash and I hadn't been working together. So I tried to keep my contact with Cal to a minimum. Let Ash deal with that. He was the one who kept on avoiding me.

Lucy took her usual spot on a plastic deck chair and started scribbling things down.

Ivy shifted from foot to foot beside me, clutching her device. "Jeez, what's taking so long? Don't Drow usually show up pretty quick?"

Just as she spoke, a Drow came straight out of the Nether. It lunged for me. I blocked his first blow and caught him in a headlock.

"Hurry up!" The Drow struggled against my grip.

"You can't be holding onto him while I use this," Ivy cried.

"Fine." I punched the Drow in the face, knocking him to the ground.

Ivy raised her device and a stream of electricity shot out of it like lightning. The Drow screamed as his body exploded into a pile of ash.

"Well, at least we know the device works," I remarked. "Don't think you're going to get samples that way, though."

CHAPTER 16

CASSIE

A month passed in a blur of classes and more patrols. And more attempts of using Ivy's new device.

Ash and I hadn't talked during that time. Even though he'd approached me a few times. From what I'd heard, his cases had been closed and there had been no more suspicious deaths so far.

My search for Avery had gone cold too. I couldn't find anything on her. It made me wonder why I'd seen her and what it had really been.

So far, I hadn't figured out what had gone wrong with my powers either. Thankfully, they'd come back a day or two after. I hadn't found anything in the archives either. None of my ancestors ever mentioned losing their abilities.

Maybe it'd been a one-off. But I'd stay vigilant.

Estelle wouldn't have warned me for no reason.

I headed to my spirit magic class that afternoon.

My phone bleeped. One message from Ash saying we needed to talk. I deleted it. Don't know why I didn't just block him.

Another message from Mike asking if I wanted to grab dinner later.

We'd been spending a lot of time together lately. He seemed eager to start dating again. I was still hesitant. Yeah, I liked him, but he didn't make me feel the way Ash did. At least things with him weren't messy and complicated like they were with Ash.

Mike had been supportive about helping me with finding Avery.

At least he supported me. I wouldn't just make up with Ash just because he didn't have cases to work on either. He left me when I needed him and wouldn't even talk about that kiss. He couldn't just come running back when he felt like it.

He wanted time apart so that's what he got.

My spirit magic class had been one of the more interesting ones that I had been doing this term. I'd never learn more than the basics of spirit magic since Estelle had always been more keen to teach me about slayer stuff.

To my surprise, Jolie sat in the class today.

Odd given how adamant she had been about not using her powers anymore.

I wondered if Gran had been lecturing her about it or if she'd had a change of heart.

I went and sat beside her. "Didn't expect to see you here."

"I took your advice. That doesn't mean I'm going back into the spirit realm." Jolie ran a hand through her long purple hair. "Why are you here?"

"I have my reasons, but it's a pretty cool class."

The teacher, Kristina Dixon, came in. She had long black hair with a grey streak through it like a lightning bolt.

"Morning, class. The last few weeks we've been talking about spirit magic and how it works. Today we are all going to be practising by summoning a spirit."

Jolie groaned. *Maybe this wasn't such a good idea,* she said in thought.

Why? You're not going into the spirit world, I pointed out.

Summoning spirits is still dangerous. You never know who or what might come through. Jolie scowled at me. *If something dark —*

Magic is all about intention. That's what Gran says.

"Since you two seem so focused, why don't you go first?" Professor Dixon's voice brought me back to reality.

Jolie and I both jumped.

"Wait, what?" I frowned at the professor.

"You two can start off by summoning spirits. You do know how to do that, don't you?" Professor Dixon put her hand on her hip.

I raised my hand and froze the class. "I thought she was cool."

"Cassie, you can't freeze the entire class." Jolie gaped at me. "What if someone sees? We'd be in even more trouble."

"Just do it. Are you gonna be alright doing this?"

Jolie took a deep breath and then let it out. "Don't think I have a choice. Why did she have to pick us to go first? We should've been paying more attention. You always had a way of getting me into trouble."

"Don't be so dramatic. You could do this in your sleep." I did a quick read-through from my textbook. "This is pretty simple. We did this as kids. Just say the spell to call the spirit. Plus, light a candle. You can't get much more easy than that."

"I never use spells. I just ask spirits to come to me."

"I think for the class we have to. Come on, try to relax. The more nervous you are the more likely the spell is to go wrong."

"What if something bad comes?" Jolie bit her lip. "Spells open the doorway for anything to come through. Damnit, I knew I shouldn't have taken this class. I should never have let Gran's lectures get to me."

So Gran had got to her. That didn't surprise me. Gran had a way of keeping everyone in line and she wouldn't let Jolie give up using her powers.

Noise filled the class again as it unfroze.

"Well?" Professor Dixon arched an eyebrow at us.

"I can't use a spell. It's too dangerous," Jolie spoke up. "I'm a spirit witch. I don't require spells."

Wow, since when did Jolie stand up for herself? It was about time. Being involved with Jared and everything that happened with his murder had shattered her confidence in herself and her powers.

"For the class, everyone needs to summon a spirit with a spell. Not all of us are spirit witches, Miss McGregor."

Jolie took another deep breath and lit a candle. "Spirit, come to me, I summon thee."

A simple spell. One Gran had taught us when we were kids. Maybe she wanted to keep things simple.

A cool breeze blew through the room.

The translucent form of a woman appeared. She smiled and waved at Jolie before vanishing.

"Good. Although it would have been better if the spirit had stayed a little bit longer and you had spoken to her." Professor Dixon nodded. "Now you, Miss Morgan."

I chanted the same spell Jolie used.

Nothing happened. Damn, why wouldn't it work? It was an easy spell — one I had used before. But not for a while though.

"Try again. Perhaps you need something more specific."

"Okay." I thought about rewording the spell. Instead, another spell came to me. So I chanted that instead.

Professor Dixon's eyes widened. "What language was that?"

Before I had a chance to answer a gust of wind hurtled through the room. Books and papers went flying.

What the hell?

"What did you do?" Jolie shouted over the

roaring wind.

"I cast a spell!" I yelled back. "This wasn't supposed to happen."

The wind picked up, reaching a crescendo.

"Make this stop!" Professor Dixon yelled but I could barely hear her.

"I don't know how." I shook my head at her.

The force of the wind shattered the windows in the doors. The magic shot out of the doorway and vanished just as quick as it had come.

I jumped up and scrambled over the piles of debris so I could get out of the classroom. I had to know if the spell worked. Although I knew I'd be in trouble for wrecking the classroom.

To my surprise, I found a woman with long red hair in the hallway. She looked bewildered.

"Who are you?" I frowned at her.

I'd cast a spell to summon Liv, not whoever the hell this was.

"I'm not meant to be here." The woman vanished in a blur of light.

Damn, who had she been and why had the spell brought her to me?

"Miss Morgan, what the hell did you do to my classroom?" Professor Dixon demanded.

I raised my hand and froze the class again.

My magic wouldn't last that long but I needed to look around. I flung my senses out like a net, searching for whoever had appeared after my spell.

"Murphy?" I called out. Usually he stayed in the forest for most of the day when I had classes.

Murphy appeared in a bright flash of light and waved his paw at me.

"Good boy. Listen, I summoned someone just now. Can you go find her and bring her back to me? I need to know who she is. Hurry, boy."

"Miss Morgan." Professor Dixon appeared in the doorway and I knew I would be in deep shit this time.

CHAPTER 17

ASH

The last month had been nothing but paperwork and filing. I knew Cal was disappointed in me, but I was more disappointed in myself.

Elora hadn't been happy to have Vikram's case closed, but without any evidence I couldn't justify keeping it open any longer. There had been nothing else I could do to convince Cal to keep the cases open.

Worse still, Cassie still refused to talk to me. Ever since the day she forced me off Estelle's property. So I hadn't had the chance to patrol either.

Cal came over to my desk. "You haven't been making magus reports for several weeks now."

Here we go. I knew this would happen

sooner or later. I knew I'd have to be careful what I told him.

"Cassie doesn't want me around." True enough.

"Why? You've been working together since you were children."

"She says she doesn't need a magus. Maybe she's right."

"Ridiculous. Slayers and Magi work together. That's the way it's always been."

I shrugged. "I can't force her to work with me."

"Did you have a falling out?"

"You could say that." I really didn't want to go into the details of why we'd fallen out, but I knew he would ask. My mind raced searching for a reasonable explanation, but I couldn't come up with one. I couldn't tell him the truth.

"Talk to her and set aside your differences then."

"It's...complicated. You and Estelle took breaks from each other."

"Yes, and look how that ended. Stop wasting your time around here and fix your relationship with Cassie," Cal snapped. "That's an order. I won't have her hurt or worse because you're both too stubborn to —"

"Talking won't fix this. Believe me, I've tried."

"Try harder. Go." Cal motioned for me to leave.

"I don't think Cassie and I can recover from this." I didn't budge.

"It's not like you to give up, boy." Cal scowled at me. "Ask yourself this, would you be able to live with yourself and the guilt if something happens to her?"

I looked away. No, I wouldn't but I didn't know how to fix this.

Could we ever go back to the way we were? Pretend like I never kissed her?

Being apart felt easier and harder at the same time.

"Go, Ash. I won't ask you again. Don't come back until you fix things."

I sighed and left. I wandered around the main campus for a while, unsure what to do. Could I just go to Cassie and ask her to work together again? She made her feelings clear already. I didn't want to make things worse. Forcing her to work with me wouldn't go over well, I paced up and down, still unsure what my next move would be.

"I can't believe she blew up the class." Elora's voice caught my attention. "Unbelievable. She'll be expelled for sure. She already blew up her dorm room."

Dorm room. She must mean Cassie or her roommates. They were the only students who had blown up their dorm so far.

"Hey, who blew up the classroom?" I moved in front of Elora and her gang of friends.

Elora sneered when she saw me. "Your girlfriend, of course. Guess she's as useless as you are."

That meant Cassie. I ignored her comment. "What happened?"

She shrugged. "I'm not in that class. Summoning spirits is for weirdos. But I heard she cast a spell and blew up the class. If this doesn't get her expelled, I don't know what will." She laughed.

"I heard Professor Dixon marched her straight to the chancellor's office." Elora's dark-haired friend sneered.

I transported out and headed for the chancellor's office. Casting my senses out, I searched for Cassie's presence. Lo and behold, she was in there.

I sent my senses out further so I could listen in on what was happening inside.

"What kind of spell did you cast?" the chancellor demanded.

"I didn't recognise the language," another

woman said. Probably another professor.

"It was just a spirit summoning spell," Cassie spoke up. "I never knew it'd cause so much chaos."

"Doesn't matter. You've caused nothing but trouble since you came to my island," the chancellor snapped. "I need you to leave. I —"

Without thinking, I shoved the door open. All three women stared at me in surprise.

Cassie threw me a glare. "You've got to be joking," she muttered.

I forced a smile. "Sorry I'm late."

"Why are you here, Agent Rhys?" the chancellor demanded.

"Because Cassie's my partner. Sorry about the little mixed up in class. We had an evil spirit to take care of."

"You were there?" The professor arched an eyebrow. "I didn't see you in the class."

"I didn't want to alert the other students to my presence. You know Cassie's secret has to be protected." I gave the chancellor a pointed look. "You can't expel her for doing her duty. The cost of damages should be covered. I think we're done here. Right, Cass?"

Cassie gave the chancellor a forced smile. "Right. Like he said, we were working."

"Working on what?" The professor wanted

to know. "Why would an enforcer even be there?"

"That's confidential and I'm not at liberty to discuss me or my partner's cases." I gave the chancellor a nod.

Cassie got up and followed me out. We headed down the corridor in silence. Then she grabbed my arm and pulled me into a classroom. "What the hell was that?" she demanded. "What are you even doing here?"

"Saving you from the looks of it." At least she'd finally said something to me.

"I don't need saving. Jesus, Ash, you're unbelievable. How'd you even know I was there?"

"Elora told me and I was coming to find you anyway. Cal's demanding we fix things between us."

She gave a harsh laugh. "You've got to be joking. Like I said we're done. I don't need a magus."

"Tell Cal that."

"Did you tell Cal why we're not partners anymore?" Cassie crossed her arms.

"No. Didn't think it'd go over well." I sighed. "Cass, I'm sorry. I don't know else I can say to you."

"There's nothing to say. It's done. You can't take back what happened. Tell Cal whatever you like." She turned to go.

"Can't we just…move past this?"

"No. I can't. Neither of us can take back what happened."

She turned away and I grabbed her arm. "I'm sorry," I repeated. "I really am. If I could take it back; I never would have given into my feelings for you."

"What happened in the classroom?" I added.

"That's not your business. You're not my magus. You're not anything."

I flinched at that. "Maybe not, but you're everything to me and you always will be."

Her eyes widened and some of her anger seemed to fade. "Just… Stay the hell away from me." She stormed out of the room.

I blew out a breath. Damn, just being near her again brought everything back to life me. Guess I missed her more than I could've imagined.

The sound of footsteps made me turn around as Cassie came back in.

She grabbed me and kissed me hard.

I didn't bother resisting her. How could I? She was everything I'd ever wanted.

I put my arms around her and pulled her tight against me. Our bodies seemed to fit together like they were made for each other.

She drew back but I pulled her in for another kiss and deepened it. She pressed her hands against my chest and shoved me back against the wall. Then she kissed me hard. I picked her up so I could get her closer to her. I ran my fingers through her hair, as she wrapped her legs around the waist.

I had to be close to her, had to feel her. Had to touch the forbidden that I had in my grasp. Maybe this was wrong but I'd be damned if I ignored it.

My lips trailed down her neck and she moaned with pleasure.

"Ash," she gasped.

The sound of voices echoed down the hall and the classroom door rattled. I gripped Cassie tighter and transported us out.

We both fell onto my living room floor.

"Ow." Cassie groaned. "What the fuck?" She landed on top of me.

"Not exactly where I was aiming for."

She slapped me hard and scrambled off me. "You're unbelievable."

I sprang up. "Hey, that wasn't all me."

Cassie shook her head. "This is why we can never go back to the way we were."

"Cass —"

She held up her hand. "Don't. Just stay the hell away from me."

CHAPTER 18

CASSIE

Goddess, I couldn't believe what I'd just done. First, I almost got expelled, then I threw myself at Ash. I'd gone completely mad.

I couldn't believe him showing up in the chancellor's office like that. Coming to my rescue just infuriated me even more. Like I needed his help. I would have handled the chancellor somehow. Would have thought of something.

Instead, typical Ash swooped in to help. He'd been doing that since we were kids.

Damn him. Why did he have to be so infuriating? And why had I kissed him?

I didn't want to be around him anymore. I couldn't believe what I had just done.

I screamed as I stormed in and entered the

North Tower.

"Hey, tryna study here." Lucy scowled at me from the kitchen table.

"Sorry. I...need to...hit something," I growled. I swear I could still taste Ash. Still smell his scent on me. Maybe I needed to shower and then go a few rounds with a punching bag.

"What happened?" Lucy got up. "Guess you saw Ash."

"I... Never mind."

"So did you kiss or what?" Lucy put her hand on her hip.

"Yes. No. I mean —"

She squealed. "I knew it."

"What?"

"That something happened and that's why you're so pissed off at him." I made a move to leave but Lucy grabbed my arm. "Oh no you don't, spill it. I've been waiting over a year for this. What did you do? Was the kiss bad?"

I gritted my teeth. "Lucy!"

"What? It's about bloody time you two gave into that sizzling attraction. I mean, Ash is gorgeous and —" Lucy grinned as I growled at her. "What? Was it really that bad?"

"No, it was...Argh, okay, fine it was good. Damned good. That's bad."

Lucy scoffed. "How could that be bad?"

"Because I swore I'd never get romantically involved with him. Look at what a complete disaster my parents' relationship was."

"Yeah, but you're not your parents. And it's pretty obvious Ash loves you as much as you love him."

"I never said that." I scowled.

"You don't have to. It's pretty obvious to everyone."

I put my head in my hands. "What am I gonna do?"

"Maybe tell him how you feel."

I shook my head and lowered my hands. "I don't know what I feel."

"You can't ignore it forever."

"I almost got expelled today. I don't need romantic drama as well."

"Did you tell Ash someone's been following you?"

"We don't talk that much. I mainly yelled at him and…vented my frustration."

Lucy snorted. "You go, girl. What are you gonna do?"

"Ash and I… We can't be together. You know the rules."

"Rules that were made up like a thousand years ago. Cass, you can't ignore this anymore. You need to figure it out."

My phone buzzed. I pulled it out, half expecting it to be from Ash.

Instead, it was Mike.

Crap. I forgot my text to him asking him to meet. I slumped down into one of the kitchen chairs. "This is a nightmare."

"Doesn't have to be. If you love —"

"Can we please stop the Ash nonsense? I blew up the classroom."

Lucy's mouth fell open. "How or why would you do that?"

"I cast a spell to summon a spirit — class requirement. Think I used an old slayer spell and it went a little haywire."

"Who were you trying to summon?"

I sighed. "Liv. Before you moan at me, I knew it was dangerous. I just wanted my sister."

"No one can blame you for that." Lucy squeezed my hand. "Have you found out who's following you?"

"No, I keep having the same vision of Liv. And someone appeared after the spell. A redhead. She seemed familiar somehow. That's why I need to see Mike. And I'll set a trap for whoever is following me. Then maybe I can figure out what the hell is going on."

I headed out to Mike's room. The place was in his usual disarray of coffee cups, piles of books scattered everywhere and dirty laundry on the floor.

"Hey, what's up?" Mike asked. "Your message sounded kind of anxious."

"I need you to do some facial recognition stuff for me."

"Is this about Avery? Have you seen her again?"

"No. Something else."

"Cass, you know you don't have to hide things from me."

"I'm not hiding anything."

Except I'm a slayer. Oh, and by the way I kissed Ash again.

I couldn't tell him either of those things. "Just something else I've been working on. You know, enforcer stuff."

Mike had been great the past few weeks, but I didn't feel comfortable sharing my big secret with him.

As for the Ash thing that didn't matter. Mike and I weren't a couple.

"I thought you weren't working with Ash?"

"I'm not. It's complicated. Can you help?"

"I wish you trusted me." Mike's shoulders slumped.

"I do."

"I kind of thought we were partners again. Like the old days."

I already have a partner. The thought shot through my brain. But I didn't, not anymore.

Mike and I had been partners once. I could never be my true self with him. I'd always held back. Just like I did now.

I didn't know what to say. I didn't want a partner. Not after everything with Ash.

"You know I trust you. You're a good friend."

"Kind of hoped I was more than that."

"Mike, I am not ready to jump back into a relationship. Besides, I have feelings for someone else."

"You mean Ash."

I looked away and shook my head. "Ash and I can't be together. It's complicated. Maybe I should go."

"No, you don't need to. What'd you need help with?"

"I need to track down every redhead female on the island."

Mike chuckled. "That's specific. What did they do?"

"I've no idea, but they showed up when I cast a summoning spell today."

"What kind of spell?" Mike sat down at his keyboard and started typing and clicking.

I bit my lip. "One to summon a spirit."

"What wording did you use?"

"Just a simple come to me spirit spell." It had been a simple spell. Just a pretty powerful one that shouldn't have conjured a living person.

I had to know who that woman was. Maybe it'd give me an idea on how to capture whoever had been following me.

"Getting through everyone on the island will take a while."

"I have time." I couldn't face any more classes today. Not after blowing up Professor Dixon's class. I settled on the chair beside him.

"Anything more specific?"

"Green eyes, pale skin. Maybe about five foot six. Pretty sure she was a witch, but I only caught a quick glimpse of her."

"How do you know she was a witch?"

I shrugged. "Just a guess."

"Let me see."

My phone rang so I answered it without looking at the caller ID. "Yeah?"

"We need to talk."

Ash. Just great.

I hung up and blocked his number. I couldn't deal with him right now.

"Who's that?" Mike frowned.

"No one. Any luck?" I shoved my phone into my pocket.

"It will take a few hours at least."

"Call me when you get a list of people." I got up. "See you later."

I used the transference stone to get to Estelle's house again. Heading out to the archives, I scoured through the books. Searching for the spell I'd used in class. There were so many to go through.

The slayer's collection on spirit magic was pretty extensive.

I went over to the pedestal and typed in the spell that I'd used and something thudded to the floor.

Turning around, I found a black leather-bound tome titled Spiritus Magicus. Grabbing it, I flipped through until I found the spell.

At the bottom of the page there was a warning not to use the spell on a living spirit attached to a body. Or there would be catastrophic consequences.

"What? Liv can't be attached to a body," I said out loud.

There was no way. Even if Liv somehow survived that warehouse explosion she wouldn't leave. Not without telling me.

Or would she? She'd kept Jared and a

whole other side of her life separate from me.

What else had she hidden?

An alarm rang out.

Not again.

Who or what had set it off this time?

I hurried downstairs to look around.

If my stalker had followed me here they'd be in for a big surprise. Intruders weren't welcome in a slayer's house.

A quick glance at the house's security screen hadn't revealed anything either.

Estelle always kept weapons around so I grabbed a sword from the hall.

The alarm kept blaring.

Come on, I know you're here somewhere. Where are you?

I raised my sword ready for an attack.

But after scouring the grounds I couldn't find anyone or anything that might have been there. Whoever it was had vanished.

CHAPTER 19

CASSIE

A few more days passed. None of my traps so far had revealed who my potential stalker might be. But I still felt like someone was following me around.

I finally gave in and tried calling Ash, but his phone went straight to voicemail. Why wouldn't he answer? Worse still, my powers had disappeared again.

I knew Ash had a lot of grimoires at his place so I figured I might find some answers there. I hadn't been able to find anything in the slayer archives.

Lucy insisted on coming with me — which relieved me in case we ran into Ash. This was her in her element around books and trying to solve a problem.

"Are you sure breaking into Ash's place is a

good idea?" she asked.

One thing I knew about Lucy - she liked playing by the rules.

"We're not breaking in. I have a key."

"But what if Ash is there? You haven't exactly been talking to each other lately."

"Maybe he can get his head out of his arse and help us."

"I'm happy to be your stand-in magus."

If anyone was good for the position, it was her. But the same time, she didn't know slayer history the way Ash did. Besides, maybe it was time we talked. What we would say to each other I had no idea.

"What are you going to do if he's in there?" Lucy added.

"He's not. He's probably too busy working on a new case. Let's find the grimoires." I headed into Ash's bedroom and glanced around. No sign of any books. Great. That meant he probably kept them at Cal's place. Argh, I didn't want to face him again. "Luce, I don't think they're here."

"We should call him and ask —"

"Which part of me and Ash still aren't talking didn't you understand?" I put my hands on my hips.

"Right. Where would they be?"

"Cal probably has them."

"Let's go and see him then."

"No way."

"Are you gonna call Ash again? Leave him a message and maybe he'll come and talk to you."

I scowled at her. "No, but Cal won't give them to me."

"How do you know that unless you try?"

"Lucy."

"Oh come on. You can talk to your dad and we'll find books. Ghost girl can sneak in with me."

I gaped at her. "Wow, you want to steal from Cal?"

"It's not stealing, it's borrowing. Plus, if you stay long enough I can find what we need without taking anything from his place."

"He could sense you."

"Not if Ghost Girl uses her mojo he won't." Lucy took out her phone and called Ivy. "She says she's on her way. Let's go."

I couldn't believe I'd let Lucy talk me into this.

"Since when do you break the rules?" Ivy asked Lucy when she met us near Cal's block of flats.

"We're bending them, not breaking," Lucy insisted. "Plus, Cass needs our help."

"Maybe I should just send Murphy to find

the grimoires. He's good at finding things."

"You're backing out." Lucy frowned at me.

Of course I was. I hated my dad. The last thing I wanted to do was talk to him.

"Murphy can't find specifics stuff in books, can he?" Lucy added.

"Not exactly." I hadn't thought of teaching Murphy to read. Did dragons even do that? He'd proven he could find Drow and other items.

"You can talk to your dad whilst we sneak around."

"Cal probably isn't even home. He usually spends all his time at the enforcers tower," I remarked. "So we won't get in."

"Yeah, we will. Or maybe we should call Mike. He's good with hacking," Lucy said. "It's early. Just knock on the door and see what happens."

I blew out a breath. "I'm not calling Mike." He'd never agree to break into the chief of enforcers' flat.

"Well, get going." Lucy gave me a shove towards the door. "We'll be right behind you." Ivy threw dust over herself and Lucy, and they vanished from view.

"Where…"

"Get moving before the cameras spot you talking to yourself," Ivy insisted.

"You two are bloody mental," I muttered. I hit the buzzer for Cal's flat and waited.

"We're helping you," Lucy insisted.

"Cassie?" Cal's voice almost made me jump out of my skin.

Great. Why for the love of all things holy did he have to be home?

Someone kicked me.

"Um... Hi. Can I come in?" Goddess, I sounded pathetic.

Murphy snoozed on my shoulders so he was no support.

Cal paused then the door buzzed open. Odd. I half expected him to question me. He knew I hated him and wouldn't want to visit him.

Reluctantly I headed inside and took the lift up to the top floor. Couldn't believe I was doing this.

Maybe we should just do some more tests at the lab, I told my friends in thought. Anything would be better than this.

We've run some tests. Told you they were inconclusive, Ivy stated.

Do more then. Hell, I'd rather be poked and prodded then see Cal.

The lift doors dinged open and I headed out.

I'd lost my mind and gone barmy. Sure, I

didn't want to talk to Ash right now but that would be better than this.

Cal, dressed in his usual tailored suit, stood by the front door.

"I'm surprised to see you. Is something wrong?" Cal asked. "Where's Ash?"

There's the million pound question, Lucy remarked. *You could have gone to him.*

Be quiet, would you? I groaned.

"I…I need to ask you some things… About Estelle." Wonderful, I just had to bring up my birth mother. But it'd been the first thing that popped into my head. What else could we talk about? Other than slayer stuff. But I couldn't think of a good excuse about that. Cal winced. "It's been eight years. Let's go over things again." I pushed past him into the flat and hope the others would have time to get through the front door to.

"What do you want to know?" Cal asked. "I thought we went over Estelle's death last term."

"What about the elf witch that Liv went after? What about the Queen of the Nether Realm?" Ash probably told him what I found out last term.

"Ash said your sister killed the witch."

I winced. "She…" I didn't want to admit my sister was capable of that. Sure, I killed

Drow, but what Liv had done had been different. I still couldn't understand why she had gone after Estelle's killer. Yeah, I wanted to find out who killed our mum and why, but I wouldn't go to the lengths she had. "What do you know? Why didn't you look for the witch?"

"I spent years looking. Finding someone in the Nether Realm is impossible."

"People come and go from the Nether, maybe there's more to it than monsters."

"Even if there is, no one can travel there without certain death."

"But you can open portals to the Nether Realm," I pointed out. "Didn't you ever go through to see what's on the other side?"

Cal shook his head. "That's forbidden. The rules are there for a reason."

"Falling in love with the slayer is forbidden too, but I doubt you're the first magus to do that. Just the first to have a kid with one."

Guys, have you found any grimoires yet? I found it weird they hadn't said anything else or called me yet.

We're looking. Goddess, your dad has a whole library in here, Lucy said in awe.

Lucy, focus!

Cal flinched. "I don't regret my relationship with your mum. Maybe it wasn't right but —

please promise you'll stop searching for Estelle's killer."

I snorted. "Why would I do that?"

"Because you've seen it leads to nothing but death. Look what happened to your sister."

I gritted my teeth. Why did I agree to this?

Lucy, hurry up. I need to get out of here.

"I knew coming here was a waste of time." I shot to my feet.

"Cassie —"

"Save it. I'll be the good little slayer and slay the bad things that come from the Nether. But I deserve to know why someone killed my mother," I snapped. "While you're at it, why don't you ask your precious Ashlan what he's been doing lately?" I turned to leave.

Cal came over and took hold of my arm. "Cassie, I'd like the chance to —"

"To what? Man up and be a father? That ship sailed a long time ago." I yanked my arm way.

"I was your mother's magus. If you need help —"

Lucy? I snapped. *Ivy?*

We need more time, Cass. This place is a minefield, Ivy replied.

We need to leave. Right now.

"I don't need your help. After everything that Ash has done, I'd be better having no magus too."

"What did he do?"

"His case is more important than his duties," I wanted to say but didn't.

"Doesn't matter," I stated.

"I thought you and Ash got along? You know better than anyone not to let personal feelings get in the way of your duties."

"Given how much you and Estelle argued, I don't think you have any right to judge." Light burst from my hand and exploded the table. "Holy crap." My powers were back. I laughed with relief.

"Before you leave, perhaps you can tell me why your friends are snooping through my library?" Cal arched an eyebrow.

My relief faded.

Shit.

"I need a grimoire. Since Ash isn't around to help." I crossed my arms.

"You could just ask. I'm your... I'm here to help." Cal shifted gears. "Which one do you need?"

"I need to know — never mind." I headed to the front door.

"Wait, personal feelings aside, you can't slay on your own."

"Estelle did."

"Yes, and look where that got her. You're not Estelle. You've only been slaying a few months. I know the grimoires better than anyone."

I hesitated. I couldn't tell him the truth but doubted I could lie either. Not to him.

"Hypothetically, has a slayer ever lost their powers?" I asked. "I had a dream — maybe a vision. I lost my strength — and everything else."

"Powers can be affected by emotions. That could weaken you. No, I've never heard of anything else affecting a slayer's powers," Cal said. "What did you see? Be specific."

"Me, powerless. Being almost choked to death by Drow."

"Visions can mean many things." Cal leaned back in his chair. "I gather you and Ash haven't resolved your issues yet?"

My eyes widened at that. Damn, I hadn't expected him to realise Ash and I weren't working together anymore. "What do you mean?" I feigned ignorance.

"Cassie, I know you've been slaying on your own. Ash hasn't handed in any magus reports in several weeks. What's going on between the two of you?"

I got to my feet. "That's none of your

business."

Cal sighed and shook his head. "Believe me, I understand the relationship between a magus and a slayer better than anyone. I know how close you can become and I know how hard it can be to ignore your feelings for each other. I'm not blind. I've seen the way he looks at you. Did something happen?"

I looked away. "Like I said, not your business. Besides, I've been coping just fine without having a magus around. Estelle was right, I don't need one."

"Your mother and I often argued with each other. Sometimes she wouldn't speak to me for several weeks, but we always came together again. We knew how important our duty to each other was. Much more important than our personal relationship. You and Ash need to settle your differences and put them aside. If you don't, he might not be there when you need him most."

I scoffed at that. "He hasn't been for most of term and I am just fine. I don't need him to hold my hand."

"No matter what's happened between you, find a way to make this work."

I headed to the door but hesitated. "How did you do it? How did you deal with Estelle being the slayer and how did she deal with you being her magus when you were involved with each other?" Odd. I never thought about asking him about his relationship with my birthmother. Most of my memories were of them arguing and then ignoring each other for weeks on end. But there had been times when we'd all been happy together, especially when I was a little kid. But their relationship had grown much more tumultuous as I'd grown older.

Weird. I never thought I'd talk to Cal like this. Despite my animosity towards him, he did understand what I was going through. He was the only one who could understand it.

Cal gave a faint smile. "No relationship is ever easy. Especially when you work together so closely. But she was my best friend and that friendship helped us overcome many things." He shook his head again. "I don't know what went wrong between us. She grew more distant from me. I know she started experimenting with different magics and pushing the boundaries of her powers more. She even talked about going into the Nether Realm. That goes against everything we'd ever been taught."

Wow, one of the earliest things I had learnt as a slayer was to never enter the Never Realm.

Was that why Estelle told me I didn't need a magus? She always encouraged my relationship with Ash. It surprised me when she had written that in her legacy statement. Yeah, I had been managing by myself thanks to help from Lucy and Ivy. But I couldn't deny I missed having Ash around. Even just talking to him. I missed our friendship.

I slumped against the door frame. "I don't even know how to begin to fix things between us. We both messed up."

"Try talking to him."

I gave a harsh laugh. "Talking doesn't usually go well. Usually we just end up arguing."

"I usually find apologising helps."

Fine, maybe it was time Ash and I talked.

CHAPTER 20

ASH

I couldn't believe another victim had been found. After a month of nothing.

Did we have a serial killer at the academy? Once word of that got out people would start leaving the island.

When I had got the news of the latest victim, my first thought had been to call Cassie. But I didn't think she would want to hear from me. She hadn't said a word to me since our last encounter.

"Not another one," Tye remarked. "I know these guys were arseholes but…"

"He's got no visible injuries either." I knelt beside the body. "Guess the same dark magic killed him. We've got to figure out what type of magic it is. Maybe you should run some tests with Ivy this time."

Was that why Estelle told me I didn't need a magus? She always encouraged my relationship with Ash. It surprised me when she had written that in her legacy statement. Yeah, I had been managing by myself thanks to help from Lucy and Ivy. But I couldn't deny I missed having Ash around. Even just talking to him. I missed our friendship.

I slumped against the door frame. "I don't even know how to begin to fix things between us. We both messed up."

"Try talking to him."

I gave a harsh laugh. "Talking doesn't usually go well. Usually we just end up arguing."

"I usually find apologising helps."

Fine, maybe it was time Ash and I talked.

CHAPTER 20

ASH

I couldn't believe another victim had been found. After a month of nothing.

Did we have a serial killer at the academy? Once word of that got out people would start leaving the island.

When I had got the news of the latest victim, my first thought had been to call Cassie. But I didn't think she would want to hear from me. She hadn't said a word to me since our last encounter.

"Not another one," Tye remarked. "I know these guys were arseholes but…"

"He's got no visible injuries either." I knelt beside the body. "Guess the same dark magic killed him. We've got to figure out what type of magic it is. Maybe you should run some tests with Ivy this time."

"Ivy Blue? Are you serious?" Tye gaped at me. "She's still a criminal."

"She's not a bad person. She's the only one who's got results so far."

"Rules are there for a reason, Ash. You don't want the case being thrown out, do you?"

"Of course not, but the chancellor will be pressuring us to get answers. Fast. Just run all the tests you can." I needed to stop holding back too. I had to get some leads on this before anyone else got hurt. Or this would no doubt be ruled an accidental death just like the other cases.

After getting a few statements, I ducked around the corner and closed my eyes.

Letting out my demon side wasn't something I did often.

The only good thing about my demon side: I could sense killers and people who had blood on their hands. I'd tried sensing things when the other two bodies were found but hadn't detected anything.

Come on, show me something.

I sent my senses out further over the island. The static from the wild magic hit me like a jolt of electricity.

The sounds of voices caught me off-guard.

Damn it, I needed to get out of there.

My wings popped out of my back (another demon perk) and I shot into the air. My glamour would keep me hidden from any watchful eyes.

I flew away from the main campus and glided towards Cassie's place at the North Tower. I didn't know if anyone would be in there, but I needed to calm down.

Damn my demon side. I hated it when it threatened to take over. Even my bracelet which repressed it did little good. I needed to find Cassie. She somehow kept me calm. Odd, given what she was. Demons despised the slayer almost as much as the elves did. It didn't matter if she wouldn't be happy to see me or not. Just being around her usually calmed my demon side down.

I landed on Cassie's balcony.

To my surprise, her doors were open. Gasping for breath, I doubled over and fought to get my inner demon under control.

Someone screamed and I almost fell off the ledge.

"What the hell, Ash?" Lucy screeched. "Since when do you have wings?"

By the Nether, why did she have to be in here? So much for keeping my demon side a secret.

"You have wings," I pointed out. "What

are you doing in Cassie's room?"

"Yeah, I'm fae and I live here. Not — what are you?"

I gripped the railing and the metal twisted in my grasp. "Where's Cassie?" I growled.

"Cassie!" Lucy yelled. "Get in here. Hurry!"

Cassie rushed into the room. "What's —"

"Ash is a demon. I think he's possessed."

"Yeah, it's no big deal. He's not possessed either." Cassie pushed past Lucy and came over to me. "Why are you changing?"

"You know about this?" Lucy gaped at her.

"Luce, chill. Ash isn't a threat to anyone." She knelt in front of me. "Why'd you lose control?"

My demon side faded back inside me. I breathed a sigh of relief. "Because I'm trying to find the killer. Another elf was found dead."

"Wonderful." Cassie groaned. "What are you doing here?" Her earlier concern vanished.

"I...came to tell you that and see if you wanted to help in the case."

"Wow, are you serious? Given what a —" Lucy scoffed. Her fear of me had faded.

"Lucy, don't you have books to read?" Cassie asked.

"Why didn't you tell me he's a demon?"

Lucy put her hands on her hips.

"Because it's not my secret to tell."

"It would have been nice to know." Lucy stalked off.

"Did you say you wanted help on the case?" Cassie crossed her arms.

"There's a third victim. But we need to keep this quiet and —"

"And what? That doesn't change anything that happened between us."

"Cal's demanding we work together again. What else do you want me to tell him?" I demanded. "I already said I'm sorry. I don't know what else I can say. Can we at least try to get along, at least for the sake of appearance?"

"So what? We pretend like nothing happened? I'm not sure either of us can do that. Can you?"

I hesitated and didn't know how to fix this. I just knew I had to try. I wanted my partner back. I wanted my best friend back.

"I'm willing to try. Are you?" I arched an eyebrow at her. "Besides, I need you. If I'm going to track down a possible killer, I'll have to use my demon side. And if I lose control…"

"Fine, I guess we can try." Her face remained impassive so I couldn't tell what she was thinking or feeling. "I don't wanna work together when you feel like it, though. Either we're partners or we're not."

"We are. I'm sorry, my demon side...has been weird."

"You could have told me." Cassie scowled at me.

"You're right. I should have." My shoulders slumped.

"Did you sense the killer then?" I took that as her acceptance and relaxed.

I'd forgotten how well she knew me. Even after seven years of being separated. She seemed to know more about my demon side than Cal did. He always insisted on repressing it. He'd been the one who'd given me my spelled bracelet. Cal'd probably vanquish my demon side if he had the chance. Cassie's birth mum tried that when I'd first changed and almost killed me. Now I never wanted to relive that awful experience again.

"I can't sense much of anything. I used to be better at sensing killers." I ran a hand through my hair. "It scared me when I was a kid. Well, until you promised to slay me."

"Maybe you're holding back."

"I don't hold back. I let my demon side take control. That usually..."

"Try again. I'll be here to stop you before

anything goes wrong."

I hesitated. I did control it once today. Did I dare risk again? Letting the demon out twice in one day was something I'd never tried before.

"Come on, nothing else we tried so far has worked." Cassie gestured for me to change.

"What about Lucy? I don't want to scare her again."

She waved a hand in dismissal. "She'll get over it."

"Let's head out to the Nether Realm's border. See if we can sense anything there."

She shook her head. "Are you mad? That area's under surveillance. Someone might see you."

"They only scan for energy readings. There's no cameras."

"Let's stay here for now. The wild magic might interfere."

She had a point.

"Okay, but be ready in case I lose control." I slipped my bracelet off again. After a few moments, my wings came out and my eyes changed colour — I knew that from experience.

Murphy looked up from where he perched on a cupboard, but he didn't move. Just kept staring at me.

I closed my eyes and let my senses roam over the island.

"Nothing," I growled. "There's too much energy."

"Maybe you need to be near the crime scenes. You can fly me there. Let's go." Cassie slipped her arms around my neck.

"You want me to carry you?"

"Yeah, I can't fly. You need me there with you. If you stay in the air, no one will see us."

Part of me wanted to protest. Being close to her reminded me of how we'd kissed. But I needed her with me. One way or another, I'd just have to deal with my feelings.

Picking her up, we flew away from the tower.

The island stretched out below us. A mass of gleaming towers and a canopy of green and brown as forest covered the denser sides of the island.

I sent my senses out and scanned the island. For all I knew the killer might not even be here. They could have come out of the Nether, but it seemed odd only Vikram's friend group had been killed. They weren't the most liked group at the academy. That's for sure. But why had someone killed them?

Everyone I talked to so far said they were arseholes. But I doubted anyone wanted to kill them. The gang tormented and bullied people. But would that lead to someone using strange magic? Why not use magic to get them to back off?

It didn't make sense.

"Are you getting anything?" Cassie asked.

"Nothing."

"Go lower. You're pretty high up. Get closer to the buildings."

"But —"

"You're glamoured. No one will see us."

I swooped lower, careful not to get too close to the tower housing blocks. "Nothing. Maybe the killer wasn't recently here or they're good at shielding themselves." I circled around the towers. "Have you found out anything about your friend Avery?"

She furrowed her brow. "You didn't believe me about that."

"I — well, did you?"

She scowled. "No. Avery's nowhere to be found. That's not unusual for her. But someone has been following me around the last few weeks."

My eyes widened at that. "Why didn't you tell me?"

She scoffed. "Why do you think? We've been avoiding each other for weeks."

I moved away from the housing blocks and

headed over to the academy's main building and food court. Still nothing. The food court was almost empty at this time of day.

"I'm not getting anything."

"Maybe you aren't trying hard enough."

"Of course I'm trying," I growled.

"Don't growl at me, Ashlan." She gave me a slap.

Odd. She didn't show the slightest bit of fear around my demon side. Sometimes I feared it would turn on her too.

"Concentrate. Maybe you need something to trigger you."

"Like what?"

"Maybe this." She wriggled out of my grasp and fell.

Holy Nether. I swooped lower and Cassie landed on the roof of the food court before I had the chance to grab her.

"Don't do that again," I snapped.

"Why? I'm fine. Slayer agility and all. Guess we'll have to try something else."

CHAPTER 21

CASSIE

Ash and I spent the next couple of days looking for clues on what had happened to the latest murder victim, but we didn't find much in the way of leads. Tests couldn't prove the cause of death either so unless we found something pretty quick it would probably be ruled as an accident as well.

"We are missing something." I paced up and down the kitchen where I'd moved my victim board to. They had pictures and information on all the different victims on it.

Ivy scowled and shovelled cereal into her mouth. "Do we have to see that while eating?" she asked between mouthfuls.

"Don't know how you can eat when she had dead bodies on there." Lucy grimaced. "Can you keep that in your room or at Ash's place?"

"Ash's place is too small. I brought it down here to see if it would give me a different perspective. I still say we need to figure out what kind of magic killed them."

Ivy perked up. "Ooh, more tests with Nether magic? I've got some equipment —"

"That didn't go well last time," Lucy snapped. "You get yourself blown up if you're not careful."

"We can skip classes and head out to the Nether. There has to be some way of testing the magic that I missed," Ivy insisted.

"What about your stalker?" Lucy asked me. "Are they still following you around?"

"Yeah, I still haven't figured out who it is or what they want."

I still got the feeling of someone following and watching even on the way to classes. So far, I hadn't seen anything but shadows and no discernible figure.

"Have you told Ash?" Lucy arched an eyebrow.

"About what?" I frowned at her.

"Being followed. Or for your feelings for him."

Things between Ash and I were tense. We hadn't talked about our relationship or lack thereof. We just agreed to work together.

Both of us were too afraid to broach the subject. To be honest, I didn't want to discuss either. But I knew we'd have to sooner or later.

"I told him about the stalker. That's all."

"Maybe he can help figure out who it is," Ivy suggested.

"We'll deal with the stalker later. Let's focus on this." I motioned to the board.

"I say you go to your mum's house. She knew the Nether better than anyone," Lucy remarked.

"I already looked in the archives. I can't find much. She talked about going to the Nether but that was it. She didn't say how or why. Other than wrote down a few vague things."

"We can't miss class. Why don't you call Ash and we'll come to help you later?" Lucy suggested.

I reminded myself calling Ash to go visit Estelle's house wasn't a big deal. But hell, it was. The place would bring back memories for both of us.

It took all my strength to call and ask. To my surprise, he agreed. Weird, I expected him to be too busy.

We agreed to meet at the transportation

stone.

"Aren't you supposed to be working on the case?" I asked when he appeared. "Or do you have any new leads?"

Ash shook his head. "None. That's why this will be a good opportunity to look elsewhere. Maybe I'll find something in the archives."

"Oh, wait, I blocked you from the grounds." I'd almost forgotten about that. "You better hold on to me." I held out my hand. "Or you'll get booted out soon as we get there."

Ash took my hand and my skin tingled at his touch.

We reappeared on the outside the house. As soon as we did, the feeling of being watched came over me.

A chill ran down the back of my neck. Goddess, who would be here?

Do you feel that? I asked Ash in thought.

He gave a subtle nod. *Yeah, someone's here.*

Damn, must be my stalker. I didn't think there'd be stupid enough to come here. Where the hell are they?

Ash let go of my hand and shot off in the opposite direction. A high-pitched screeching sound rang out and Ash doubled over in pain.

Damn, that would be the house's security.

Typical. I should have come here earlier and removed it before I asked him to come over.

I hurried over to him and sensed someone leaving. "Are you okay?"

"Never mind that. You need to find out who's here."

"Too late, there are already gone." I grabbed his hands. "Told you not to let go of me. Come on, we need to get inside." I yanked him back to his feet.

"Why would anyone follow you? How would they know about this place?"

I shrugged. "No idea. Let's go."

Once we reached the tower, I let go of his hand but Ash gripped it again.

"I'm sorry, I should have —"

"Don't. Just don't. We can't change what happened. Let's just move on."

"We have to talk sometime. We can't ignore this thing between us."

"Ash, we need to work together. That hasn't changed. And we're better together. Let's not ruin that." I turned away from him. The last thing I wanted was to talk about this.

"We can't pretend we don't have feelings for each other."

"Nothing's changed. I'm a slayer, you're my magus. Us being together will only get in the way of that."

"So what? We just ignore this thing between us?"

"We have to. Now can we focus on our duty?"

Geez, I couldn't believe he'd brought this up now. The very thing I'd been avoiding and dreading.

Why couldn't he just agree to ignore our feelings and move on? That was better for both of us.

I headed up the steps and into the archives. Pulling up the security system, I scrolled through the list of approved people. My name and Liv's name appeared at the top of the list. Seeing her name felt like a punch to my chest.

Wait, Estelle and Liv were barely speaking to each other around the time Estelle died.

"Ash?" I called out for him.

"Yeah?" He came up the stairs. "Listen, about what I said..."

"Forget that. Do you remember much about what happened when Estelle died? I thought she barred Liv from the house. They argued about something that day."

Ash frowned. "I remember they argued. Didn't think she locked Liv out, though. Did she?"

I shrugged. "I can't be sure. Estelle's death is a jumbled mess in my head." I motioned to the screen. "How could Liv have been here again? The house was sealed up."

"Maybe she came back after Estelle died."

I shook my head. "Mum said the day after Estelle died the entire place was locked up. Liv wanted to come here but Estelle's legacy statement said that neither of us would be able to come back until we were both of age. So why is her name on here?"

"I don't know. Wait, you don't think your sister is still alive, do you?"

"I don't know what I believe anymore. I didn't think Liv would ever leave me but…" I tailed off. "Now I don't know."

"There's probably a reasonable explanation. Let's get searching."

I tried to focus on searching for stuff but my mind kept going back to Liv.

Why was her name on the system? Was she the one who had been here? The alarm hadn't gone off. That meant someone on the approval list had been here.

Unable to concentrate, I went back to the screen to check the records of who had been here.

Only my name appeared on it.

"Damn it."

"Did you find something?"

"No." I sighed. "No, never mind. Keep

searching."

Ash turned away from the shelves he'd been scouring through. "Where's Estelle's grimoire?"

"What?" His question brought me out of my agonising thoughts over Liv.

"Her grimoire. If she went into the Nether, she would have written it down."

I shook my head and pulled the book down. "Here. There's nothing much in it. Mostly vague accounts and her talking about my training."

"That's not it."

"What?" I stared at him, confused.

"That's not her grimoire. Not the real one."

"What do you mean?" This book had to be Estelle's grimoire. It was the only one I found up here.

"Come on, Cass. We used to sneak a look at her grimoire all the time when we were kids. It drove her mad." Ash smiled at the memory. "This is her official one, not her personal one."

It took me a second to realise he was right. How had I forgotten that?

"Where did she keep it then?" I furrowed my brow but no memory came to me.

"Only you and Estelle would know that. She always kept it well hidden and never told anyone where it was."

"I can't remember. You know how jumbled my memory is."

"Your memories are there. You just need to concentrate. Maybe you can trigger a vision." He took hold of my hands. "Close your eyes."

I really didn't want to feel him this close to me. My breath hitched as my skin tingled. "Nothing."

"Concentrate."

"Ash, you know my visions don't work very well. I can't just call one on demand."

"Estelle thought you could. Maybe you just need to relax." He let go of my hands and came up behind me. "Concentrate," he whispered in my ear.

He was so close, heat radiated of his body and I could feel every hard inch of him.

"This isn't working. I can't trigger visions." I pulled away from him and put some much needed distance between us.

"Try harder."

"You really need to make your mind up," I growled.

"What do you mean?"

"One minute you're supportive, now you're being an arse. Which one is it?"

"Cass —"

"Don't Cass me. You —"

"At least I'm not ignoring my feelings. Is this what it's gonna be like? We ignore our feelings for each other?"

"Do you have better idea?" I held up my hand. "Forget that. It doesn't work between us. It can't. So we just need to move on."

"Fine."

Fine, was that it? I didn't know what I'd expected. Something. We couldn't be together. We both knew that.

"You could try harder," Ash added. "Those memories are still inside you."

I hesitated. "What do you remember about…that day?"

He knew what I meant. The day Estelle died.

Ash looked away. "I try not to think about it."

"Why?"

"Because I thought I lost you that day and in some ways I did." Ash came over and sat beside me. "We need to figure out how to trigger your memories."

"Did we really used to sneak looks at her grimoire?"

"Yeah, don't you remember?"

I shook my head. "Everything is blurred." Then an idea struck me.

Estelle would have known about my blurred memories.

That grimoire had to be around here somewhere. I went over to the pedestal and looked round to see if there were any recorded messages left on it. Like the one Estelle had left for me the first time I'd come here. But I found nothing.

"Where did we used to go to find her book?" I asked.

Ash shrugged. "She moved it around a lot and hid it in different places. Are you sure you don't remember much about the days before she died?"

I shook my head. "I'm sure. It's all a jumbled mess. Did we look at it again before that day?"

"Maybe a few weeks before. I can't be sure. You were always the one who suggested we look at it. You always got excited when she was working on something big." Ash leaned back on his chair. "What has triggered them so far?"

I shrugged. "Things come to me every now and then. Bits and pieces but nothing substantial."

"Maybe we should try some magic. A spell. Come on." He took my hand and led me out to the other room.

This room was different since it had been used for spell work. A huge silver circle took up most of the floor.

"You really think a spell will help?" I said, unconvinced.

"Maybe even meditation. We need to try something. Plus we've been doing spells together since we were kids. It will be just like the old days."

The old days. When we'd been in training and he'd been my closest friend. We had been so attached to each other Estelle said we were like siblings. For most of my life he had been my other half. The one person who understood me. At least until we'd been separated. At times it felt like that between us again, especially over the last year. Up until our feelings for each had messed everything else.

"Don't fall in love with each other." Cal always warned us of that when we were kids. Ironic given his relationship with my mother. But maybe he hadn't wanted history to repeat itself.

Sometimes I wished we could go back to that. Yeah, my feelings for him had been there for a long time. What was I supposed to do about them now?

I pushed those thoughts away. We needed

Estelle's grimoire. She had knowledge of the Nether. Things I couldn't remember. Things that might helped with the case and everything else that had been going on for the last few months. I still had no idea what her message meant.

I kicked off my shoes and stepped into the circle. Static charges against my skin. "Wow, this brings back memories. Estelle made us sit in here for hours until we got our spells right."

"See, you can remember." Ash grinned.

"It's just a flash. I don't remember everything." I shook my head, disappointed.

"You went through a lot that night." Ash pulled his boots off and stepped in the circle too. "Just try to focus on what you want to remember."

We both sat down, just as we had when we were kids. He reached out and took hold of my hands.

I tried to ignore the close proximity between us.

Focus, Cassie. You're here to remember things.

"I have no idea what kind of spell to cast." My mind went blank when I thought up possible verses for a spell.

"I know a magus spell. It's to reveal repressed memories, but I've never tried it on anyone before. I think it was to help slayers in times of need. Cal always said it was unpredictable."

"Cast it. We need that grimoire." I gripped his hand tighter.

Ash began reciting a spell in elvish, the words low and melodic. I closed my eyes as energy shifted around us and dragged me in.

I focused on the grimoire and what I wanted to see.

"Cassie, are you even listening to me?" Estelle demanded.

I flinched and realised we were standing in the archive room. Estelle's leather-bound grimoire clutched under her arm.

"Yes, Mama."

"Good, now I need you to keep this safe. You must remember where it is. You'll need this when the time comes."

"What do you mean, Mama?" My twelve-year-old self frowned at her. "Why won't you be here to show me where it is?"

"Because…" Estelle sighed. "Because one day you'll be the slayer, not me. And you'll need to be ready. There are forces that seek to destroy you. Some of them will come for you. When you become the slayer, I won't be there to protect you. Trust no one, not even those closest to you. Trust no one but yourself."

I shuddered at her words, but she turned away and put the book down. She held up her hand and a fireball appeared. "Remember the knowledge is here when you choose to find it." She threw the fireball at her grimoire and it exploded in a blast of light.

CHAPTER 22

CASSIE

The memory of Estelle burning her grimoire shifted until I found myself in a dark room. The sound of raised voices echoed down the hall. What the heck? Who the hell was screaming?

Shadows blurred around me and everything distorted.

"Cassie, I'm sorry to have to do this…" Estelle's voice sounded far away.

Then I heard screaming and a crashing sound.

I gasped as I broke out of the memory. To my surprise, I found myself lying on the floor. My heart thudded in my ears and my head throbbed with pain. "Ash!"

"It's okay, just try to breathe."

I clutched my head. "Argh, you never said this would hurt."

"It shouldn't. What did you see?"

"I…" The pain intensified and voices echoed in my ears. "Ugh, make it stop, make it stop!"

"Cass, it's okay. I told you this spell can be unpredictable."

"My head…" Tears flowed down my cheeks and I sobbed harder. "Do something."

Warmth radiated over me as I felt Ash's healing energy but it did nothing to ease the pain.

Ash came over and wrapped his arms around me, cradling my head in his lap. "It's okay. It will pass. I'm right here."

"Don't leave me. Don't let me go." The sudden feeling of him leaving overwhelmed me. I didn't know if it was a warning or something left over from my jumbled memories.

"I won't. I promise. You know I'd never leave you."

"You did before, you left me. You let me go. I wanted to you to come back and you never did," I carried on rambling. "You promised me you wouldn't leave. I remember… I was hurt after Estelle…left.

You came and found me. You promised you wouldn't leave!"

"I won't. That won't happen again." He stroked my hair as I cried harder. "I only left because you needed help. I had to get Cal. After that, they took you away. I never got to see you again. They wouldn't even tell me where you'd gone."

"Promise me you won't leave again."

"I swear it. You know I'd never leave you. It's okay. It's just lingering memories. I told you the spell could be intense. You're just feeling your past emotions."

"Am I? It feels so real. Like it just happened." I clung to him. "Can we ever go back to the way we were?"

"Yeah, like you said we can move on. We can…" his voice broke. "We have to. It doesn't matter what happened between us. I'm yours and you're mine. That's the way it'll always be."

"She burned it…"

"What?" Ash stared at me, confused.

"Estelle burned the grimoire. I saw it. I think… I think she knew. It's like she was prepared. Do you think she knew she was going to die?"

"I don't know. Maybe. But if she knew, she would've done something. That woman was invincible. That's what I always thought. I never believed a few Drow could take her down."

"She burnt it," I repeated. "She said I had to remember, that'd I'd need it when I became the slayer."

"So the book still exists somewhere?"

I shook my head. "I don't know. It's all blurred." I pulled away, missing the feel of his embrace. "Maybe we need to try again."

"No way."

"Ash, come on, I need to remember more."

"I can't. There are a whole bunch of warnings that go along with that spell. The first being don't use it again right after."

"But it worked. Come on, the pain's subsiding. Please."

"No. I'm not putting you at risk."

"Fine, then I guess I'll have to get them another way." Jumping up, I slipped my shoes back on and hurried back into the archive room.

"What are you doing? Maybe you should rest a while longer."

"Estelle was in here when she burnt the grimoire." I closed my eyes, willing another memory to come to me.

"Cassie, come on wake up, don't leave me," Ash's voice rang through my ears.

"What happened to me the day Estelle died? You never talk about it." I turned around to face him.

"That's because I don't like to think of it." Ash shoved his hands in his pockets. "You got hurt, I found you. I thought…I thought you were dead. You weren't breathing and you had a pretty bad head injury. Blood was everywhere. I couldn't heal you and my magic wouldn't work."

"You begged me to stay. Said you'd never let me go. I heard you." I touched my face, almost feeling his past self cradling me. "Did Cal heal me?"

"No, you woke up but you were out of it. That's why I went to get Cal."

My shoulders slumped. "Why can't I remember more? She knew I'd need the grimoire. Why didn't she tell me where to find it?"

"It'll come back. Don't try to force it." Ash came over and slipped his arm around me, pulled me back into his arms.

I clung to him. He had always been my rock growing up. He still was. It felt good to ignore the tension between us and just feel the good stuff for once.

"Are you still mine?" I asked him.

"Cass, I've always been yours. You know that."

I reached up and kissed him, softly at first, then pulled him closer as I deepened the kiss. A flash of something went through my mind of the book and I pulled away.

"Hey!" Ash protested. "Why did you stop?"

"Because…" I waited for the memory to reveal more but nothing came to me. "Damn it. I think Estelle put the book somewhere."

I scoured through the shelves and found nothing.

"If she left the book here, where would she hide it?" Ash asked.

"It could be anywhere."

We searched the place further but no more memories came to me.

I headed back to class the next day. My mind still reeling. Ash refused to cast a memory spell again for at least a few days. Typical. I knew what I could and couldn't handle. We needed that book.

As I headed down the corridor, I sensed someone watching me again. But this time it was Ash.

I hurled a ball of purple light at him. "This is called stalking, you know." My magic blasted him against the stone wall.

"Ow! How did you know I was here?"

"Because I can sense you and you're not that stealthy. Not to me anyway."

"I was cloaked."

I crossed my arms. "I can still feel you. I can sense you. You didn't answer my question."

"I was trying to find out who is following you."

"They won't follow me with you around," I pointed out. "And it's too crowded in here for them to follow me. And it's usually in secluded areas. Don't you have a case to work on?"

"Not exactly. They're ruling that an accident too."

"Unbelievable." I rolled my eyes. The elves were more stupid than I thought. "I have to get to class."

"Any more memories about the grimoire?"

I shook my head. "Nope. Maybe it's time to cast a spell again."

"I already told you —"

"Yeah, yeah. You worry too much. See you later."

After class, I headed outside.

I hope you know what you're doing, Ash said in thought.

We'd planned on seeing if anyone would follow me outside. With Ash and Murphy at a distance.

I can still feel you, I pointed out.

How? I'm cloaked.

Because I can. It's easy to sense you. At least for me it is.

You shouldn't be able to.

You sense me too, don't you?

Ash hesitated. *Yeah, I do. A lot more than I'd like.*

Sorry my presence bothers you so much. I scoffed.

Cass, that's not what I meant.

Shush. I need focus. I kept my senses on alert as I headed down the alley.

Don't go that way. I can't see you, Ash protested.

You can sense me. That's enough.

Cass, I don't like this.

I ignored him. One way or another I'd find out who been following me. Somehow, I thought it might be Avery, but I couldn't imagine why. Why wouldn't she just come out and talk to me? It made no sense.

I took my phone out and pretended to be listening to music.

Come on, stalker. You have to be around here somewhere.

I carried on walking until I came to a dead end.

Cass, what are you doing? Ash demanded. *We agreed no dead ends.*

No, you agreed. I leapt into the air and jumped over the eight-foot wall. *I'm not making this easy for them.*

Just stay where I can see you.

Wow, my guardian elf. I rolled my eyes.

I walked up and down the different alleys between the housing blocks. It took a while before the feeling of being watched came over me again. And it wasn't Ash or Murphy.

I notice my stalker always backed off whenever I had Murphy with me. So I'd told him to stay with Ash.

"Ow!" I pretended to trip up and dropped my phone. The presence behind me grew stronger. I spun and threw a crystal at whoever was there.

Light expanded, blinding me as the crystal's magic took hold.

Thank you, Ivy. Her new invention had come in handy.

"Avery?" I gasped when I caught sight of her. "What the hell? You're the one who's been following me?"

"Cassie, look. I'm sorry for being all stalker-ish. You need to let me go."

"No, not until you explain what the hell you're playing out. Why follow me around for weeks? Is this the same kind of game?"

"I'm sorry, Cassie." Light shimmered around Avery.

"Oh no, you don't." I rushed forward and made a grab for her.

The light intensified and swept us both away.

"Cassie," Ash yelled.

I gasped as we reappeared, surrounded by grey mist. What the hell?

"Oh, shit. You're not supposed to be here." Avery gaped at me. "You have to leave."

I crossed my arms. "Not until you tell me why you've been following me. Where the hell are we?" I glanced around, uneasy.

"We're in Limbo. Listen, there's a lot you don't know but I can't tell you —"

"You can and you will. Jesus, I thought you were my friend."

"I am. That's why I've been watching over you all term."

"That makes no sense. Why would you do that?"

"Like I said, it's a long story. I'm sorry, Cassie." Avery vanished in a flash of light.

Unbelievable. She'd left me in Limbo with no way out.

CHAPTER 23

ASH

I jumped down into the alley where Cassie had vanished. The crystal trap still hovered in place. I had no idea where she disappeared to.

"Cassie?" I called out for her again. "Cass?"

Nothing.

Murphy hovered beside me and made a skittering sound.

"Can you find her, boy?"

Cassie mentioned about Murphy moving between realms and how he had no trouble finding her. Murphy continued making strange sounds.

"Murph, I need you to take me to Cassie. Can you do that?"

Murphy flew around the spot Cassie had disappeared in. His distressed sounds grew. Like he couldn't figure out how to reach her.

By the Nether, I should have reacted faster. I should have — never mind.

"Come on, Murphy. We'll get her back."

I shimmered out with Murphy and reappeared in her room at the North Tower. There had to be a way to bring Cassie back. I wasn't about to lose her.

But I didn't know where to begin. The first rule of being a magus was never to lose sight of your slayer.

"Murphy, I need you to sense Cassie and find her for me."

Murphy flew around my head, chirping and clicking.

If he couldn't find her then I'd have to. I grabbed Cassie's brush off her chest of drawers. Maybe a spell would work.

I chanted something in the elvish language. Nothing.

Curse it.

I kept hold of the brush and headed downstairs. To my relief, Ivy and Lucy were there.

"Ivy, could someone transport out of your trap?"

"No. Why do you look so worried?" Ivy narrowed her eyes.

"Cassie vanished. We found Avery. Cassie questioned her, but they both disappeared."

"That's impossible. I designed a trap to hold energy. Nothing can escape from it." Ivy shook her head.

"Wait, didn't Cassie say something about Avery being a spirit witch?" Lucy asked. "Maybe she went into the spirit world."

"Good, but I have no way of getting there."

"Jolie might be able to help," Lucy pointed out.

Ivy scoffed. "She's afraid of her own shadow nowadays."

"She has to. Thanks." I shimmered out.

I reappeared in Jolie's dorm room.

Jolie yelped. "Good goddess! Who…?"

"I'm Ash, Cassie's magus."

She put her hand to her chest. "Oh, right. What are you doing here?"

"Cassie's missing. I need you to take me to the spirit world. I think she might be trapped there."

I'd met Jolie a few times growing up and a couple of times last year, but I didn't know her that well.

"Why —"

I held up my hand. "Never mind. Just take me there. I need to get her back."

Jolie shook her head. "I can't."

"Don't give me crap about not using your powers anymore. Your cousin is missing. You have to help me find her."

"You don't understand. I can't. The spirit world is a vast place. There's no guarantee I —"

"Cassie and I are connected to each other. Please, Jolie. I can't lose her. I won't."

"You really love her, don't you?" Her eyebrows rose.

I nodded. "Yeah. Please just take me there."

Jolie sighed. "Alright. I hope you're right." She took my hand.

Light blazed around us as we transported out. The world shifted. A huge glowing archway appeared up ahead.

"What's that?" I frowned.

"It leads further into the spirit world. The further you go the harder it is to come back," Jolie warned. "Do you sense her?"

I cast my senses out. "No, we need to go deeper." I walked off and headed towards the archway.

"Ash, wait." Jolie ran to keep up with me. "You have to stay near me. You could get lost —"

Pain pierced through my skull and growling inside my head echoed through my ears.

"Ow, what's happening?" I sank to my knees and clutched my head.

"Goddess, this can't be good. Come on, we need to leave." Jolie reached for me.

"Stay back." My voice came out low and guttural. My body flashed as it tried to shift.

"Ash, what's wrong with you?" Jolie backed away. "I-I think something is trying to possess you."

Her words drifted away. I'd never felt my demon side this strong before. What was wrong with me?

"Jolie…can demons enter here?"

"No. Demons aren't allowed here. What's —"

"You should go. If I lose control —"

"Are you a demon?" Jolie asked.

"It's a long story. Go! I'll find her."

"I don't think she's here."

Light blurred as Murphy shot towards me.

Murphy knocked me to the ground, digging his claws into me. He growled and held me down.

"We need to go. Cassie isn't here," Jolie insisted.

"You don't know that," I growled. "I need to explore."

"Ash, you can't stay here. We need to go and get help. You need to be rid of that demon."

I gave a harsh laugh. "That's not possible. I've had this since I was a kid. It's part of me."

Jolie gasped. "I-I have to go." She vanished in a flash of light.

Wonderful, I couldn't believe she'd just left me here. Cassie said her cousin had no backbone. She was right. I didn't think she would leave me, though.

How would I get out of here without help?

"Murph, look around this place and see if you can see find Cassie." Murphy didn't budge. "Come on, go and look for her. I'll wait here."

Still he refused to move.

"Go, Murphy. Find Cassie."

Still growling, he dug his claws in deeper and light blurred around us. We reappeared in the archives Estelle's house.

"Why did you do that?" I demanded. "I told you to find Cassie."

Murphy flew into the air. "Cass, Cass." Murphy chirped.

"Cass? Where?"

Murphy vanished and reappeared a few seconds later, dragging Cassie with him.

"Whoa." Cassie stumbled and Murphy wrapped himself around her. "Easy, boy. I'm happy to see you too."

I groaned and clutched my head. My wings were out now and the demon in me fought for control.

"Ash, what's wrong? Why are you changing?" She came over with Murphy still wrapped around her.

"Jolie took me to the spirit realm. It brought out my demon side."

Cassie shoved Murphy away and knelt in front of me. She gripped my hands. "Hey, it's okay, I'm back."

All at once my demon side receded.

I pulled her to me and wrapped my arms around her. "Where did you go?"

"Avery dragged me into Limbo. I can't believe she left me there. What a bitch! Are you okay now?"

"Yeah, I think Jolie left me in the spirit world."

Cassie pulled away and gaped at me. "What? Why?"

"She didn't like my demon side. She knows about me now."

"We'll worry about that later. I can't believe Avery is my stalker. She says she's been watching over me."

"Why?"

She shook her head. "No idea. She wouldn't answer my questions. I think I might know where Estelle's grimoire is now."

CHAPTER 24

CASSIE

I banged on Jolie's door a few days later. She'd been avoiding me since she left Ash in the spirit world. But I wouldn't give up so easily. "Jo, come on. You know I won't leave until you help me. Plus, you left Ash for dead. So I'd say you owe me big time." I banged again. "I know you're in there."

I hadn't had any luck trying to find the grimoire either. I'd had a memory of it being in the spirit world. That seemed a good place to hide it but so far, I hadn't found anything when I went there.

Jolie blew out a breath as she opened the door. "I really need to learn to say no to you. What do you want?"

"I need you to help me find someone. Another spirit witch like you. Her name is Avery Devlin."

"I told you I don't do that anymore. So please stop harassing me." Jolie shook her head.

I pushed past her into the room. "Look, Jo, I know you went through a lot when Jared died. But you can't give up on your gift."

"It's not a gift. I don't want anyone else to get hurt."

"Think of all the good you could do. That outweighs the bad stuff, believe me."

Jolie shook her head again. "No, Cassie. I can't."

"Can you just do this me this one favour?"

"No. Because you'll ask me for help the next time you have a problem."

"Fine. I didn't want to have to do this, but I guess I'll just have to go to the other side by myself." I pulled out a potion vial. I'd brought this with me as a backup in case she refused to help.

"Wait, what's that?"

"It's poison. Stops my heart for a couple of minutes. Well, at least until my slayer healing brings me back. Hopefully." I pulled the cork out of the bottle. "You know Ash will go ballistic if anything bad happens to me."

"Wait, you can't poison yourself," Jolie gasped.

"I don't have any other way of getting to the other side. Spells don't work and you won't help."

Jolie crossed her arms. "You could have told me your boyfriend's a demon."

"He's not my boyfriend." I wasn't sure what he was anymore. More than a friend, I guess. "He's only part demon and he controls it. It's not his fault. He gotten bitten by one when he was a kid. Even Estelle knew about it."

"Estelle let a demon be your magus?" Jolie stared at me wide eyed.

"He's not a demon. He's mostly elf. Now will you help or not? Or do I have to poison myself?"

Jolie sighed. "I hate you."

"Does that mean you'll help? Because if I die, you'll have my death on your hands. Mum and Gran will never forgive you for that."

"Fine. I'll take you, but this is the last time." She grabbed my hand and lights blazed around us.

We reappeared surrounded by heavy mist. "I always expected the other side to look welcoming and peaceful," I remarked.

"This is Limbo. Not the other side. Spirits pass in and out of here," Jolie replied. "I can't believe I let you talk me into this."

"I know, I've been here before. How do we find Avery?" I asked. "Could a spirit witch stay here for prolonged periods?"

Jolie shrugged. "I guess you could. I never stay long. It's too risky." She used her free hand which glowed with light. "Avery Devlin, come before us." We waited but no one appeared. "What makes you think she's here?"

"I haven't found her anywhere else. Plus, I don't see how she could have stayed on the island undetected." All of my messages had gone unanswered and unread. Still couldn't understand why she wouldn't tell me why she'd been watching over me. We were friends yeah, but we weren't super close. She must be sneaking in and out of the spirit world to get on and off the island or else she would have been detected by now.

"Avery?" I called. "Are you here?" I pulled my hand away from Jolie.

Jolie yelped. "Don't. I need to keep hold of you or we could get separated." She grabbed my hand again.

"Okay, let's get moving then. I need to search for Avery." I tugged at her arm.

"She'd come if she heard my call."

"You've barely used your magic in the last few months." I wanted to pull away and explore. Instead, I dragged her with me. "Avery, it's Cassie. Are you here?"

I hadn't just come here for Avery. I'd come to look for the grimoire too. But so far, nothing came to me. Could someone else have found it? That seemed unlikely. I knew Estelle. She wouldn't leave her most prized possession lying around for strangers to find. But if she had put it here, where was it?

I cast my senses out. Nothing. If the book was here, then I could feel it.

So I tried a spell instead.

A shadow shot towards us.

"We need to go." Jolie turned to leave and grabbed my hand.

The shadow shot towards us and knocked us both down. Jolie lost her grip on me and screamed as a blonde-haired elf materialised. "It's about time you came back." He sneered at her. "I've been waiting a long time for you to come, JoJo."

It took me a moment to recognise him. Jared Ryland. The necromancer who'd been killed. The guy who started this mess last year. I should have known he'd be hanging around since no one had been held accountable for his death.

"Hey." I leapt up. "Back off, dead man."

Jared's eyes narrowed on me. "You must be Liv's little sister. Guess I'll have fun playing with you too." He laughed.

"How about this?" I hurled a blast of purple light at him and he staggered away from Jolie. Interesting. I didn't know my power affected spirits.

"Jared, leave her alone. I swear I never meant for anyone to get hurt." Tears filled Jolie's eyes.

"You and that bitch cousin of yours got me killed. Too bad she's not here for me to get revenge on. Guess you and the sister will have to do."

"I said back off." I stepped between him and Jolie. "Unless you want to see how I can destroy spirits."

Jared sneered. "Your powers don't work here, little girl." I hit him again. This time he howled in pain.

"Come near my cousin again and I'll obliterate you." More light flared between my fingers. "While we're here, tell us who killed you."

This could be my one chance of finding out who really killed this piece of shit.

"Your sister."

"Bollocks. Liv would never have killed you, even if you deserved it. Who else was there?"

"Why would I tell you anything?"

"Because you'll never move on unless you deal with whatever's holding you back." Jolie sniffed and got up. "You don't want to be stuck here forever. Tell us the truth, who really killed you? Have you been tormenting Liv's spirit?"

Jared snorted. "Liv's isn't here. And you're all responsible for what happened to me."

"Who stabbed you?" I demanded. "Why was there no knife at the scene? Lucy and Ivy escaped. Liv and Jolie were knocked unconscious. So who else was there?"

"That damned demon hunter."

"And where's Liv?" I demanded.

"Maybe she moved on," Jolie suggested.

Jared scoffed. "She's never been here. Some redhead killed me. Came out of the portal I opened."

"Why would Liv even want to work with you?" I said more to myself. "Why was she so desperate to find out about Estelle's death?"

Jared gave a harsh laugh. "You're joking, right? Wow, you didn't know your sister well at all. She was obsessed with finding out what happened to your mum. Even managed to find her grimoire. Got to say there's some impressive stuff in there. But most of it was hidden. Even Liv couldn't read most of it."

I narrowed my eyes. "How do you know about the grimoire?"

"He's telling the truth," Jolie said. "At least I think he is. He believes it at least."

Jared smirked. "Of course I know. Your sister complained about it all the time."

"Where's the book now?" I demanded. "Who's the demon hunter that killed you?"

"No idea. Liv kept it with her. The hunter never told me her real name. Just told me to call her Hunter."

I questioned him further, but he wouldn't give me any more answers and Jolie kept insisting we needed to leave so I finally relented.

Liv was never here. What did that mean?

My mind reeled as we reappeared in Jolie's dorm room.

"What the fuck just happened?" I asked. "How did Liv have our mum's book?"

"He wasn't lying," Jolie said. "At least I don't think he was. I know when spirits lie."

"Who's the redhead, though?"

"Ivy and Lucy claimed someone else came through the portal," Jolie pointed out. "And took the murder weapon. We don't know who or what might have come through. It could have been anything. Witch, demon, vengeful spirit."

"Well, we better find out. I can't believe he came after you."

"That's why I never wanted to go back. I can protect myself in the physical plane. But there…" She shuddered. "He's too strong."

"Jo, you're a McGregor. You can fight him. Better yet, banish him." Too bad I hadn't found Avery but instead I had been led back to Liv's case. And I'd gotten a clue about the grimoire. But I'd been through all of Liv's things. The grimoire hadn't been among them.

"I can't. He's too strong." Jolie shook her head.

"I can help you. Maybe I should vanquish him."

"No, Cassie. All spirits deserved to find peace. Even bad ones. It's best I don't go back."

"You can't let that bastard win. He used you the same way he used Liv. Banish him, but don't walk away from your gift."

"It's not a gift. It's a curse," Jolie snapped. "I won't use it anymore."

"Then why still come to the academy?"

"Because-because I'm trying to find my place now. It's not as a spirit witch."

I didn't know what else to say to her. What could I say? I couldn't force her to use her powers if she didn't want to.

"You helped me get some answers — even if they weren't the ones I was searching for." I sighed. "Just wish I could finally get a lead on Avery."

My phone vibrated and I answered the call. I'd reluctantly told her about my run in with Avery. She wasn't happy. "Hey, Mum. Find anything?"

"I found an address under Avery's alias. She changed her surname to Michaels. It's here in Colchester. I'd go and check it out, but I have surveillance work tonight."

"Text me the address. I'll check it out. Thanks." I hung up and my phone beeped with the text. "I'd better get going."

"Can I come?"

My eyes widened. "Really?"

"I-I don't want to be alone. Not after…"

"Let's go." I pulled the transpo bracelet Mum had given me last term out of my pocket. I hadn't had the need to use it until now.

"Where did you get that?"

"Mum got it for me. Let's go." I figured having Jolie with me might help since she and Avery had similar powers.

We reappeared outside a block of flats. I pressed on Avery's number and waited.

Goddess, let her be here.

"Avery walked away from her magic too," I told Jolie. "You have that in common."

"Why?"

"Her family got killed by a Nether monster."

I buzzed again but no one answered. So I tried other flats until the outer door finally opened.

We headed up to the third floor and I knocked on the door.

"Avery, it's Cassie. Are you in there?" I called out. The sound of someone moving around made my ears perk up.

"Avery?"

Still no one answered.

To hell with it. I kicked the door off its hinges. It revealed a living room with broken items scattered around the floor.

"Avery?" I called out again.

Something silver shot through the air. I ducked as a knife embedded in the wall behind me.

"Cassie," the redhead gasped.

With this the redhead Jared mentioned?

She had pale skin and dark eyes. It took me a moment to realise she was the same redhead that I summoned that day in class. The one who appeared when I tried summoning my sister's spirit.

"Who the hell are you?"

"I'm... No one." The woman turned and bolted into the next room.

"Stay here," I told Jolie.

"Wait, there's something not right with that woman's energy," Jolie called after me.

The bedroom had been ransacked too. The window that led to the fire escape stood open and the blind banged against the wall.

No sign of Avery here.

"Jo, look around the flat for Avery," I told her as I ducked out the window.

Red, as I decided to name her, sprinted off down the alleyway.

I jumped off the fire escape and landed in the alley. Then sprinted after her.

How did that woman know my name? Odd, she almost looked like she knew me. I'd never seen her before.

Could that be Avery? Maybe she'd used a glamour? No, I could see through glamour magic.

Red ducked and dashed around different alleys. She pulled something out and a massive bin blocked my way. Really?

I jumped straight over it and carried on running. *You can run but you can't escape,* I thought.

When I stopped to get my bearings, I dialled Ash.

"I think I found Jared's killer," I puffed.

"What? Who —?"

"No time to explain." I jumped over another bin.

This was getting tiresome. Did she really think she could outrun me?

Red glanced back and scowled. Tendrils of smoke shot from her fingers. A blast of magic flung me to the ground.

Red leapt onto the wall and scarpered.

How could she move so fast? Few supernaturals had the power to move at speed.

I jumped over the wall.

Murphy? I called for him. *I need you. Come here.*

I had no idea if he'd be able to cross back into the human realm but I had to try.

Fine, if Red wanted to play, I could play too.

I hurled a blast of purple light at her. She dodged it.

Come on, Murph. I need you. Now! Nothing.

More shadow magic came at me.

"Really? Do we have to waste time doing this?" I growled and ducked under her magic then blasted her again. This time she slammed into a wall.

Red yelped then sprang to her feet. She leapt onto a wall then jumped, grabbing onto the side of the building.

Jumping onto the wall, I made a leap at the building.

Shadow magic hit me and knocked me off balance.

I missed the building and fell. With a yelp, my fingers caught the wall. By the time I regained my footing Red had vanished.

"Unbelievable." I groaned as I headed back into Avery's flat to find Jolie. "The bitch got away from me.

"Are you alright?" Jolie frowned at me.

"No, she had strength and speed that were unusual."

"Maybe she's a Fey Guardian."

I shook my head. "There's only a couple of them left. She wasn't a fae. And I didn't sense any shifter energy. Witches don't move that fast."

"Maybe a demon or something from the Nether then."

"No, I would sense that. What did you mean when you said her energy was weird?"

Jolie shrugged. "I don't know — it didn't feel right somehow. Like the energy didn't belong in the body."

"You think she was possessed?"

"I can't be sure since I didn't touch her."

"Let's look around. See if we can find any clues here." I picked up some books. They were marked with the stamp of the community college. "Could Avery have been in that body?" I asked. "But I don't see how Avery could move like that."

"To me, she felt like a witch. Just… Different somehow."

"Plus, I don't see why Avery would run from me."

We scoured through the living room and kitchen. Why would anyone ransack this place? Nothing had been stolen — though it was hard to tell. The TV still stood above the fireplace.

Heading into the bedroom I rummaged through stuff on the floor. Something caught my attention. It was a photo of Liv from a couple of years ago.

Why would Avery have that?

I picked up an album and family photos. Some were of Avery and Liv together.

How well did Avery know my sister and where was Avery?

More importantly, who was Red?

CHAPTER 25

ASH

My heart raced as I headed to the North Tower to find Cassie. I'd been worried when she called me earlier to tell me about Jared's killer.

"What happened? Are you okay?" I asked when I found her in the kitchen.

"I'm fine." Cassie had her laptop perched on the table and tapped away on it. "I went to Limbo with Jolie and found Jared's spirit. He told me a redhead killed him, not Liv. And Mum found Avery's last address where I found the redhead."

"Whoa, slow down. Why were you in Limbo?" I held up my hands to stop her.

"To find Avery. Jared's spirit attacked us. So I had a little chat with him. You know, slayer to dead guy," she explained. "Avery's flat had been ransacked. Now I need to find Red — the woman I saw in the flat. She's the same woman who appeared when I cast a summoning spell."

I made her go over everything again so I wouldn't miss anything. "Any idea who Red is?" I asked.

She shrugged. "No idea. But she knew my name. Weird."

"You sure you don't know her?"

"Positive. I'm coming up with an image of what she looks like."

"How?" I furrowed my brow and leaned closer to the screen. "Cass, please tell me you're not using enforcer's software. How did you even — never mind. It's better if I don't know."

"This is her." She turned the laptop to face me. "Can you run it through facial recognition?"

"We haven't got that."

"Ash, don't bother lying. I know what the Elhanan does and doesn't have."

I blew out a breath. "You don't need to run it. I know her. Well, of her. She's a demon hunter and she's wanted by the elves and fae. Her methods are pretty dangerous. Her name is Callie Wilson. She's a witch and obsessed with killing demons. Her family was killed a while back."

"Witch, huh? I didn't think a witch could have strength and speed like that."

I shook my head. "I wouldn't say she had strength or speed. No more than the average witch. Jada and I tracked her down last year, but she escaped."

"Why would she be in Avery's flat?"

"No idea. Did you find anything there?"

"Yeah, pictures of her and Liv. Which is weird because Liv never met Avery — or at least I don't think she did," Cassie said. "Also, why would this Callie woman kill Jared?"

"You don't know if that's who Jared meant."

"There aren't many redheads with knives wandering around Colchester. I need to track her down. I'm afraid something's happened to Avery."

"Did you report Avery missing to the police?"

"Mum's gonna call it in to the local police. Not that they can do much. Avery's place looked like it had been empty for a while."

"I'll check it out later. There's one member of Vikram's gang left, and I want to keep watch on her. Wanna come?"

"I guess I can help. At least until I get a lead on Callie."

We headed off to do a stakeout and sat on the roof of the housing block.

Cassie fidgeted beside me. "Who's that girl we're watching?" She glanced at the picture. "I don't remember a girl hanging round them."

"She's one of the other victim's sisters. Her name's Nella. I don't know if she'll be the next victim, but we need to get a step ahead of this killer." I positioned the camera by Nella's open windows so we could see straight into her room, as she lay on her bed watching something on her laptop.

"You sense anything?" Cassie asked.

I shook my head. "Nothing."

"Maybe you should use your demon self again. See if you can feel anything."

I slipped my bracelet off and let my demon side fully emerge. My senses became heightened, and I scanned the building. "Nothing."

A scream tore through the air as a shadowy figure appeared in Nella's room. Something blasted her off her bed.

"No." Cassie jumped over the side of the roof and landed on the fire escape.

I shoved my bracelet back on and hurried after her. I found Cassie by Nella's body when I got into the room.

The shadow retreated out of the window and leapt off the fire escape.

"Come on!" I called at Cassie. "She's gone. We can't help her now."

My wings came out and I flew down, grabbed Cassie and flew after the shadow.

"I can run, you know," Cassie grumbled.

"How did that thing kill her so fast?" I growled.

"It hit her with some kind of shadow magic. Hurry, before we lose track of him."

I beat my wings harder and swooped lower. "How do you know it's a male?"

"I don't. You go around while I chase him." Cassie wriggled out of my grasp and jumped.

I hated it when she did that.

She landed and tackled the killer to the ground.

I swooped lower. The killer jabbed at Cassie, then leapt up and ran.

The smell of blood hit my nostrils and I froze. "Ash," Cassie gasped, clutching her chest and her hand came away bloody.

"Oh, crap." I made a move to go to her.

"Forget about me, go after the killer."

"But —"

"Just go!"

Gritting my teeth, I flew off again. Everything in me screamed at me to go back and help her. My demon raged inside my mind. It wanted out.

I'd lost sight of the killer. Damn it, where had they gone? Reluctantly, I let my demon side out and flew faster than I'd ever flown before.

Catching the killer's scent, I zeroed in on it.

He had gone past the housing blocks and somehow got to the other side of the island.

Damn it. They were headed for the wild magic.

I flew faster, I had to get there.

Light flashed around me as I shimmered out.

Shooting towards him, I grabbed the killer.

He shoved me away, his face still hidden then he dove into the wild magic.

Fuck!

How had he got away?

It didn't matter. I had to get back to Cassie.

I teleported back and found her slumped on the ground.

Damn, what had he done to her?

She was a slayer. She had healing powers. Sure, most large wounds wouldn't heal on their own but…

"Cass? Cass, are you okay?" I sank my knees beside her.

She didn't respond.

I held my hands over her abdomen. Light radiated from my palms, but the wound didn't close over. By the Nether, why wouldn't my powers work?

Lifting Cassie into my arms, I reappeared at the North Tower.

"Hey, what are you doing?" Ivy asked when she walked into the sitting room. "Is something wrong with Cassie?"

"She's been stabbed. Get the healing kit. Hurry." I put Cassie down on the sofa and ripped off part of her T-shirt. I held my hand over the wound again but still it wouldn't close.

Ivy ran back in with a box full of healing supplies. "What happened?"

"We found the killer. Press down on her wound." I took out my phone and called in about Nella's death. Then I called Cal to let him know what happened to Cassie and told him I needed help and she was injured.

"Shouldn't we get her to the healer?" Ivy asked.

"That's my job. I don't understand why my powers won't work."

Ivy pressed the cloth to Cassie's abdomen. "She needs a healer."

"There's one on the way." I tossed my phone onto the table then ran my hand through my hair.

Lucy came in and gasped. "What…"

"The killer stabbed her. Damn it, I knew I should have kept her out of this."

"I doubt you could have kept her away." Lucy touched my shoulder. "What should we do?"

A knock came at the door.

Lucy rushed over to open it.

I took over from Ivy and kept the pressure on Cassie's wound.

"I am Alia. Cal said you needed a healer." A pink haired winged fae came in.

"Hurry."

Alia came over and put a hand over Cassie. "I sense dark magic in her. She's been poisoned with it." Her hands glowed with light. "I'm not sure I can heal this."

"You have to. You can't just let her die," I snapped.

"I've never felt magic like this before." Alia pressed her hands over Cassie's wound.

"You can't just let her die," I repeated.

"I'm sorry, Ash. I don't know how to heal this." Alia's face became drawn. "The best I can do is bandage the wound and give her something to slow the bleeding. Make her more comfortable."

"Maybe we should move her to a healing wing on the main campus," Lucy suggested.

Cassie opened her eyes. "I'm not going to a healing wing. I'm staying here."

"You need to rest." I squeezed her hand. "We'll fix this."

CHAPTER 26

CASSIE

I couldn't believe I'd let the killer get the drop on me like that. He moved so fast I had no time to react. Now I'd been poisoned, and no one could heal me.

Alia bandaged me up and gave me a foul-tasting potion that she said might slow down the poison. Then she left.

Lucy hurried off and came back with her arms full of the books. "Hang on, Cass. We'll have you up and kicking arse again in no time."

"Ow, don't make me laugh." I groaned. "Where's Ash?" I figured I'd better conserve my energy, so I didn't use my senses.

"He went to see Cal."

"Great." I cringed. "I don't want to see him."

"If he can save you —"

I snorted, then winced as pain stabbed through me. "If Ash can't heal me, he can't either."

Ivy came in. "Here. Drink this." She handed me a potion vial.

"What is it?"

"A potion to slow down the poison's descent. It might buy us some more time. But first I need a sample of your blood."

"Why?"

"To test the magic. Getting it from a live source might help me come up with a way to combat it." She stuck the needle in my arm.

"Ow. You could've just use blood off my ripped T-shirt or something."

"I need to avoid contamination." Ivy drew back. "You better not die."

"It's not part of the plan."

"Good. Just... Rest, okay? You've got to hold on." She squeezed my hand. "We'll fix this."

I slumped back against the sofa. "Sure we will." I forced a smile.

"We should call your mum," Ivy suggested.

I gaped at her. "What? No way. She'll freak out."

"So we tell her when you're dead then?" Lucy frowned.

"I don't want to worry her."

"She deserves to know, especially after what happened to your sister. Maybe she can help since your family is pretty powerful."

"Having my mum and Cal here will only lead to more arguments. Just focus on finding a cure." I lay back and Murphy came over and lay beside me. He knew something was wrong. He pressed his body against mine and blue light flared around us. "Murphy, what are you doing?"

Lucy and Ivy rushed over. "I think he's drawing the poison out of you," Ivy gasped.

"Dragons can't do that." Lucy shook her head.

Black smoke poured out of me.

"Oh, goddess, he's drawing the poison into himself. Murphy, stop!" I pushed him but he wouldn't move.

"Don't stop him. Let him help. Dragons are resilient."

I didn't care. I wouldn't Murphy die instead of me.

Murphy wouldn't budge and the weight of his body held me down.

"Get off me!"

Lucy tugged at Murphy, then yelped when he snarled at her.

"Luce, be careful. You might get poisoned," Ivy said, then ran off and grabbed something from the kitchen. She re-emerged holding a hand vacuum and sucked all the black energy into it.

After a while the light around Murphy faded and he snuggled against me.

My wound hadn't healed but with the poison gone I felt better now. "Thanks, boy." I wrapped an arm around him. "You saved me." My eyes snapped shut as a vision jolted through me.

A shadowy figure stood with Red and a flash of silver came down as he was about to stab her.

"Ow!" I clutched my head. I rarely had visions and now couldn't be a worse possible time.

"I've got to go. I think I know where the killer is." I couldn't move with Murphy on me.

"You can't go. You still have a gaping hole in your chest," Lucy protested.

"Murph, get off me." I winced as I pushed him away. "Someone help me up."

"You need to rest."

"I can't rest when someone's about to get killed. Callie isn't the killer. She's the next victim. Now come on, Murph, or I'll —"

"You can't go. You could make your wound even worse." Lucy came over and she and Ivy helped get me up. My legs almost gave out from under me.

"Luce, twist my bracelet and —"

The front door banged us open as Ash rushed in. "What are you doing up?" He panted.

"I'm cured. We need to find the killer before he…" My legs gave out on me then.

Ash caught hold of me. "What? How?"

"Murphy got the poison out of her, but she still has the stab wound," Lucy explained.

"You need to teleport us to Colchester right now. The killer's going after Callie. Let's go."

"Go? You can't go anywhere. You lost a lot of blood," Ash protested.

"You can take me or I'll get there myself. Either way I'm going."

"You're a bloody nightmare," he muttered and picked me up.

I held onto him as he teleported out.

I don't know how you expect to stop the killer in your condition, Ash said as we reappeared in Avery's flat. *Are you gonna lie there and bleed out?*

Fine, you can stop him. I'll stand and watch. I rolled my eyes.

Ash helped me onto the sofa. "I'll look around. Don't move."

"Not much chance of that happening."

"Don't scare me like that again." Ash leaned down and brushed his lips against mine. He pulled away before I had a chance to react.

Ash headed off into the other room.

Was this the place I'd seen in my vision? It happened so fast I couldn't be sure. Murphy appeared beside me and purred.

Grabbing onto him, I pulled myself up and he helped me to creep across the room.

"There's no one here." Ash frowned when he reappeared in the doorway. "I said —"

I held up a hand. "I know what you said."

A scream rang out from somewhere outside.

Ash rushed back to the window and went out onto the fire escape.

I wanted to yell at him to wait for, but I couldn't slow him down.

Holding onto Murphy I made my way across to the window.

"Murph, I need you to grow big and carry me."

Damn stab wound. Murphy grew and I fell onto his back.

He shot out the window. Ash was fighting the killer in the alley below.

Callie lay a few feet away. I slid off Murphy. Pain stabbed through me, but I ignored it.

"Are you okay?" I stumbled over to her.

"Cass, you're hurt."

"Do we know each other?" I frowned at her.

She scrambled into a sitting position. "Yeah, it's me. Liv. Look, I can't really explain but…"

I furrowed my brow at her. "Liv?" I fell as my legs gave out again.

Callie caught hold of me. "Sissy, it's me. I don't look like myself but it's me."

Sissy. Only Liv ever called me that.

"But how? I thought you were…"

"It's a long story, sis, but not here. Ash can't know about me. I'll tell you everything. Meet me at Mum's house once you're healed. Call for Avery. She'll hear you." Callie raised her hands and smoke swirled over my stab wound then she vanished in a flash of light.

Liv was alive. My sister was alive and in another body.

I made some lame excuse to Ash about Callie vanishing. I don't know if he believed me or not.

He managed to heal me but whoever attacked Liv got away. He hadn't been able to identify who it was.

I still reeled from the fact Liv had been alive this time and hadn't approached me. Or told me the truth.

If I hadn't caught her, would she have told me?

It didn't matter.

I'd called for Avery more than once over the last few days. So far, she hadn't answered. I wanted answers and I wanted them now.

"Liv?" I called out as I approached the front door.

I didn't want to step foot in this place. Didn't want my awful memories of Estelle's death to come back.

Maybe they wouldn't. Or maybe I'd just have to deal with them.

"Liv? Avery? If you can hear me, come out."

Callie appeared in a flash of light. Or should I call her Liv?

It didn't look anything like Liv. Not even her eyes. They'd been blue but now they were green. No purple hair, no wings. Was this my sister?

"Thanks for coming," Callie said.

"Thanks for finally turning up." I crossed my arms. "How do I know you're really my sister?"

"Because I know you, sissy. You can fight better than anyone. You broke your arm when you were seven. You hate eggs."

"That doesn't prove anything. You could have watched me. You could have tortured Liv's spirit."

"Avery saved me. She was there at the explosion. She's the only other person I told about what happened. Cassie, look at me. I may not look like myself, but I'm Liv Morgan."

I stared at her hard. "If that's true, why would you go to Avery instead of me?"

"Because..." Callie sighed. "Because I couldn't tell you. I started remembering things about Estelle's death. It made me question everything." She flicked her hair off her face. Something Liv had always done as a nervous habit.

"She was my mum too. I lost her as well. You should have told me." I scanned her with my senses.

Liv. I'd know my sister's energy anywhere.

"You didn't remember. You didn't even seem like you cared. Nina became your mum and you seemed to forget about Mama."

"Nina has always been more of a mum to us. You and Estelle were always at loggerheads. I thought you hated her."

"I resented her. She wanted me to be a slayer. But I didn't. So I hid my powers. Pretended I didn't have the slayer genes." Liv scoffed. "She believed it. I loved her. She was our mother and I never believed that bullshit story about her being killed by a few Drow. She was too strong for that."

"You think she left?" It was my turn to scoff. "Why?"

"Think, Cassie. Remember. She worked with the Nether. She did things no slayer ever did because she thought she could conquer it. She planned this."

"Is that what you got involved with Jared? To prove she left?" I stared at her in disbelief. "If she did, she didn't give a damn about us, Liv."

"What if she can't come back? What if she's trapped in the Nether?" Liv reached out and took my hands. "That's why I spent nearly two years trying to find her and find a way into the Nether. This is why we have to find out."

I yanked my hands away. "Did you kill Jared or was that Callie?"

"That was Callie. Before I took over her body. Listen —"

"Do you even hear yourself? People have died and got hurt all for your quest to find Estelle. How many more people are going to get hurt?" I demanded. "What happened to Callie? Did you kill her too?"

"No, she died and Avery put me in her body before I could move on. Cass, I need you." She gripped my shoulders. "Together we can get through the Nether and find —"

"You've gone completely bloody mad." I shoved her hands away. "I won't help you do anything."

My head spun. I never imagined my reunion with Liv would be like this. She'd lost it in her obsession about Estelle.

"How can you not care about what happened to our mother?" Liv demanded.

"Because I never idolised her the way you do. She taught us to fight, to slay. She never acted like much of a mother. I remember more now. I unlocked my memories."

Liv stared at me, incredulous. "And how can you accept she might be trapped in another realm and not want to help her?"

"Because if it's true, she left us. I was twelve when she left me alone."

"She made sure you were taken care of."

"I can't listen to this bollocks anymore." I took off and headed back down the steps.

"I'm not the only one who's been watching you." Liv hurried after me. "Someone else has been following you around. Who else do you think has been causing deaths on the island?"

I spun around and narrowed my eyes at her. "How do I know that wasn't you?"

"Come on, Cass. You know —"

"The Liv I knew doesn't exist anymore. Why should I believe you?"

"Because I can help you catch them. They're killing people and stealing their energy."

"How do you know that? The tests never —"

"Come on, Cassie. We both know the Elhanan didn't do nearly enough to find out how those people died."

She had a point.

"How do you know how they were killed?" I frowned at her.

Liv sighed and a leather-bound book appeared in her arms. "Because Mama talked about it in here."

She held it out to me and I reluctantly took it. "How did you even get this? Mama —"

"Left it for you, I know. But I was listed in her legacy too. It took me a while but I found in Limbo. Here at the house."

I flipped open the book and browsed through the pages, until I came to one on people being drained and how to drain them using shadow magic. I read further as more and more text and images appeared.

"Geez, have you seen all of this stuff? She talks about harnessing the wild magic."

"Really? You can read those parts? There are in the old slayer language."

"Yeah, I actually paid attention to my lessons."

"Read the front of the book."

I flicked back to the first page. It read: *Cassie, be careful. Not everyone will believe I'm dead. They will come after you. Some who can wield the Nether's power just like I do.*

"What does this mean?" I asked. "The killer's here for me?"

"Yeah. Has anyone attacked you recently?" Liv asked.

"Other than being stabbed? No. Only Drow attacks. Vikram's gang attacked me at the start of term."

"Nothing else unusual?"

I frowned, unsure if I should tell her. "I lost my powers a couple of times."

"How?"

I shrugged. "I don't know. I just became weak and…"

"Because they wanted you to be weak. If Avery and I hadn't been watching you, they would have done far worse."

"How are you and Avery –?"

"We met by chance and she's…my girlfriend now."

"What?"

"It just sort of happened. I wouldn't be here without her. She saved my soul." Liv smiled. "Cass, we can catch this killer. We just need to work together."

CHAPTER 27

CASSIE

Liv seemed convinced we could lure the killer out using her as bait. I didn't like that idea but doubted I could stop her.

I didn't like not telling Ash about what was going on either. I couldn't tell him about Liv. Not yet at least.

I hope this worked. I still didn't understand why the killer would come after me.

Was it because I was the slayer? Did they want my powers?

Nella had already been taken into protective custody or so Ash told people. News of her death hadn't got out yet.

But Liv had disguised herself as Nella and walked around the campus a few times to show the killer she was around.

I really hate this idea, I told Liv. I sat perched on the roof with Murphy while she wandered around the alley between the different housing blocks.

Noted. But I am the oldest and I get to decide — Liv stopped. *Do you sense that?*

Someone was close by.

Be careful. You cannot die on me again, I warned her.

Chill, sissy. I'm a slayer too, remember?

Yeah, how could I forget? Still don't know why you didn't tell me about that either.

Because… Liv sighed. *Because I never wanted to be one. But I accept it. Now let me concentrate.*

I fell silent and kept my gaze on Liv as she headed further down the alleyway towards Nella's housing block.

Come on, where are you?

The killer had to be around here somewhere.

See anyone? I asked.

Liv didn't answer and carried on walking.

A shadow moved towards her and lunged for her.

Liv spun and punched the killer in the face. The cloaked figure staggered. Then they raised their hand and dark light curled around their fingers.

I jumped from the roof and kicked them to the ground.

Their hood fell back and revealed their face. "Mike?" I gasped.

"Holy shit," Liv said. "Isn't that your boyfriend?"

"Ex-boyfriend," I corrected. "Mike? I don't understand. How could you be the killer?"

"Not here." Liv slapped some cuffs around his hands. "Now you're powerless."

Liv transported Mike and I back to Estelle's house. Liv shoved him into a sealed spell circle so we could question him.

"I won't tell you anything," Mike growled.

His face seemed harder. Unlike the geeky Mike I thought I'd known.

"You don't have to." Liv pulled back his sleeve revealing a black scythe tattoo. "You're a reaper."

It took me a second to realise she didn't mean a Grim Reaper. Someone who took the souls of the dead to the other side.

Reapers. They were sent to kill slayers. Some said they even worked with Drow.

I'd heard stories about them but never thought they might be real.

"Wait, were you sent here to kill me?" I demanded. "Is that why you dated me?" Goddess, I thought I'd be sick. "Was that even real or some sick game to you?"

"He was sent to watch you until you became a slayer no doubt." Liv scowled. "Who are you working for?"

Mike shook his head. "No one."

"Bollocks. Someone must have sent you," Liv snapped and pulled out a knife. "I can always force the answers out of you."

"Whoa, wait, Liv." I grabbed her arm and led her out of the room. "What are you doing? We don't torture people."

"Why not? He's a killer." Liv scoffed.

"Because we're slayers, we're not like him."

"We need answers."

"Let me talk to him. We were involved. Maybe I can —"

Liv shook her head. "No. You'll let emotion get the better of you."

"Just let me try. I can handle him." I headed back into the other room. "So why did you come here? Why kill all of those people?"

"You wouldn't understand. You're too wrapped up in your little slayer gig," Mike sneered. "Just like you were when you were a PI."

"As if you care, I was just a job to you, right?" I demanded.

Mike looked away. "No, you weren't."

I crossed my arms. "So tell the truth. Why are you here?"

"I'm a reaper but I was sent to watch you. Not hurt you."

"Is that when you tried taking my powers away?"

Mike shook his head. "I needed you out of the way whilst I gathered power. Plus, I thought I could maybe take your powers but it didn't work."

"Power for what?"

"To get back through to the Nether. To go home."

"The Nether Realm is your home?" I frowned at him.

"Of course. All I want this to go home. You must understand that. I'm half human, half Drow. I don't belong here."

Liv came in and motioned for me to follow her out.

"Please tell me you're not buying his bullshit story," Liv added, once we were out of the room.

"I think I believe him. We're slayers, we can sense the truth."

"Or maybe you want to believe his crap."

"I don't. Believe me. I can't believe I dated him, let alone…" I shuddered. "What we going to do with him?"

"He's a reaper. We do what slayers have always done and kill him."

"Liv, you can't be serious." I gaped at her. "We're slayers, not murderers."

"Slayers kill reapers. If you don't have the stomach for it, I'll —"

"If he's half human, you'd be no better than he is."

"What do you suggest we do? Let him go? Because that's not happening."

"I have a better idea."

Liv wasn't happy about me calling Ash. But having Mike banged up for the rest of his life would be justice enough.

I didn't care what Liv said. I wasn't about to kill him.

"You've got a lot of explaining to do," Ash said when he appeared and frowned at Callie. "Why is she here?"

"Liv's back. She's in Callie's body," I told him.

His mouth fell open. "How…"

"Long story. Just get him out here." Liv crossed her arms. "Before I change my mind."

"Okay, still not sure how I'm going to explain this." Ash rubbed the back of his neck.

"Just say you caught him following Nella or IDed him. All that matters is you caught the killer," I said. "Good thing the Elhanan don't ask too many questions."

"Well, I do." Ash scowled. "We'll talk later."

Ash headed into the sealed room and brought Mike out.

"Cassie, please. You can't let them do this," Mike pleaded.

"Believe me, an Elhanan prison is a kinder fate than what I had planned for you," Liv snapped. "Leave my sister alone or I'll —"

"No, you have to let me go back through the Nether."

"So you can run back to your boss? Dream on, mate." Liv laughed.

"No. You don't understand. Estelle sent me to watch over you," Mike protested.

My eyes widened. "Liv's right. You are full of bullshit."

Liv glared at him. "Why would our mum send you? You're a worthless —"

"Because she trusts me. She knew people would come after Cassie when she became the next slayer."

"Where is she then?" I demanded. Not sure I believed him or not.

"She's in the Nether. You can go there and talk —"

"Let's get moving." Ash grabbed Mike and shimmered out.

"You think what he said is true?" I asked. I then realised Liv had vanished. "Liv?"

Holy shit. She must have taken what Mike said seriously.

I transported out using my bracelet and reappeared close to the Nether Realm's boundary.

Liv pressed herself against it.

"What the hell are you doing?" I called out.

"If Mama can get through, so can we."

"What? No! People don't come back through the Nether."

"Cassie, don't you want to see Mama again? Talk to her?"

"No, not if it costs us our lives. I don't want to lose you again."

"Then you better come with me." Liv pushed through the boundary and vanished into the Nether Realm.

EPILOGUE

ASH

I reappeared outside the Nether Realm boundary, surprised when Cassie called for me. I barely had time to get Mike to the enforcers tower and tell them that he was a murderer. I was supposed to be dealing with that but I knew I couldn't ignore her call.

Cassie stood staring at the boundary; pale faced. "Liv went through."

"Are you serious?" I gaped at her. "Why —"

"She believed what Mike said. I can't believe she just walked through." She pushed her hair off her face. "I have to go after her."

"What? No. No way." I went over and grabbed her shoulders. "If Liv wants to —"

"Ash, I can't leave her there by herself. If

she's right, there's a way back."

"What if you can't? What if you get lost there? I'll lose you." I shook my head. "I meant it when I said you're everything to me."

"And I can't lose my sister again. Not when I just got her back. I have to go. I promise I'll come back." She reached up and kissed me. "When I do, I promise we'll talk. Maybe we can have a real date and figure out the thing between us."

"I'll hold you to that." I caressed her cheek. "You better come back to me."

"I will. Just take care of Murphy while I'm gone." She gave me one last kiss before she turned and walked into the Nether Realm.

It left me wondering if I would ever see her again.

CONTINUED IN BOOK 3

If you enjoyed this book it would be great if you could leave a review. For more news about my books sign up for my newsletter on tiffanyshand.com/newsletter

ALSO BY TIFFANY SHAND

ELFHAME ACADEMY SERIES

Elfhame Academy Prequel Collection

Elfhame Academy Book 1

EXCALIBAR INVESTIGATIONS SERIES

Touched by Darkness Book 1

Bound to Darkness Book 2

Rising Darkness Book 3

Excalibar Investigations Complete Box Set

SHADOW WALKER SERIES

Shadow Walker

Shadow Spy

Shadow Guardian

Shadow Walker Complete Box Set

ANDOVIA CHRONICLES

Dark Deeds Prequel

The Calling

The Rising

Hidden Darkness

Morrigan's Heirs

ROGUES OF MAGIC SERIES

Bound By Blood

Archdruid

Bound By Fire

Old Magic

Dark Deception

Sins Of The Past

Reign Of Darkness

Rogues Of Magic Complete Box Set Books 1-7

ROGUES OF MAGIC NOVELLAS

Wyvern's Curse

Forsaken

On Dangerous Tides

The Rogues of Magic Short Story Collection

EVERLIGHT ACADEMY TRILOGY

Everlight Academy, Book 1: Faeling

Everlight Academy Book 2: Fae Born

Everlight Academy Book 3: Fae Light

Everlight Tales Short Story Collection

THE AMARANTHINE CHRONICLES BOOK 1

Betrayed By Blood

Dark Revenge

The Final Battle

SHIFTER CLANS SERIES

The Alpha's Daughter

Alpha Ascending

The Alpha's Curse

The Shifter Clans Complete Box Set

TALES OF THE ITHEREAL

Fey Spy

Outcast Fey

Rogue Fey

Hunted Fey

Tales of the Ithereal Complete Box Set

THE FEY GUARDIAN SERIES

Memories Lost

Memories Awakened

Memories Found

The Fey Guardian Complete Series Box Set

THE ARKADIA SAGA

Chosen Avatar

Captive Avatar

Fallen Avatar

The Arkadia Saga Complete Series

ABOUT THE AUTHOR

Tiffany Shand is a writing mentor, professionally trained copy editor and copy writer who has been writing stories for as long as she can remember. Born in East Anglia, Tiffany still lives in the area, constantly guarding her work space from the two cats which she shares her home with.

She began using her pets as a writing inspiration when she was a child, before moving on to write her first novel after successful completion of a creative writing course. Nowadays, Tiffany writes urban fantasy and paranormal romance, as well as nonfiction books for other writers, all available through eBook stores and on her own website.

Tiffany's favourite quote is *'writing is an exploration. You start from nothing and learn as you go'* and it is armed with this that she hopes to be able to help, inspire and mentor many more aspiring authors.

When she has time to unwind, Tiffany enjoys photography, reading, and watching endless box sets. She also loves to get out and visit the vast number of castles and historic houses that England has to offer.

Printed in Great Britain
by Amazon